THE AMERICAN

A MAN'S LIFE

DAVID CLAIRE JENNINGS

The American: A Man's Life

Southern Heart Publishing Co.
Author's website: www.davidclairejennings.com

ISBN-13: 978-0-9974601-6-2
ISBN-10: 0-9974601-6-4

Also by David Claire Jennings:

After Bondage and War
Hanna's Promise: A Story of Grace and Hope
Collected Essays on Americanism
The Goodness of Alzheimer's

i

For those who came before and taught me-

Lincoln, Twain, Tyson, Foote and Webb

Foreword

Following *After Bondage and War* and *Hanna's Promise*, this is the completion of a trilogy.

The structure of the book will appear to the reader as a novella with a central character telling a personal story in linear time progression from beginning to end. At least that is how it will appear throughout most of the book, with the exception of some looking back by the story-telling character.

At the end of the book, the reader learns that all that appeared present was past. At the final moment the reader will be engaged and see that the structure was indeed circular and that the end curved around to meet the beginning.

My earlier novels, particularly *After Bondage and War*, brought me to this. It became apparent David Wexley's story needed to be told. He was an American for his time and place in the American story. His life informs us of what it used to be like – how it was.

Since this is more of a novella, its focus is narrower and is concerned with just thirteen years of his life. For that period, the sub-title of this work might also be – A Man of the Gilded Age.

That term, The Gilded Age, actually came from the novel by Mark Twain of that title written in 1873. In Twain's novel, the fictional character Senator Dilworthy - "the golden-tongued statesman" – was taken from the actual Kansas Senator Samuel Pomeroy who wrote the railroad purchase clause in the Kickapoo Treaty essentially stealing the land from the Indians. Pomeroy was one of several men like Thomas Clark Durant, Jay Cooke, Salmon Chase and others, who were instrumental in the corruption and financial larceny associated with the creation of the Union Pacific Railroad via the Pacific Railway Act of 1862 and subsequent legislation.

As for the Scots-Irish, James Webb informed me and I informed David Wexley. If the fictional character, David Wexley, in this novel had been a real historic figure, this work would have been an academic work with the figure as a primary source telling a first person history as a personal biography of what he had seen, experienced and done. It could have been so because in either case, he tells the reader just how it was in his time.

And even those authentic non-fiction historiographies have perspective because as Shelby Foote has reminded us "the truth is the facts we love."

- DCJ

Contents

Prologue

What happened to him the thirteen years after he disappeared to go west, before his casket brought him back to Cincinnati on the train?

He had not found a settled life, or even what he was looking for, not even by the time he was fifty five in 1887. He saw the worst of it and it affected the rest of his life.

Men had talked to him about glory. He had heard about it and dreamed about it when he had gone to be a soldier. Ever since man held a spear and fashioned a sharp-edged weapon, he longed for glory. Homer wrote of it epically and he read it. He believed in it but learned that glory is a false God in the end.

Those years he was a man in the Gilded Age but not of it. Others were making fortunes by nefarious means. He was still trying to sort out the troubled past – to make what meaning he could out of it and get by.

America had disappointed him and there was little source of solace. The great men he had known, or known of, had made his country as bad as they had good. For many it looked like America wasn't a country; it was a business.

There was the economic Panic of 1873 resulting from government patronage and abuses in the Union Pacific railroad development. There was carryover debt from the Civil War and troubles with bonds and paper currency. The efforts to tie all this economic lunacy to the soundness of gold had failed too.

He was a man of little import in the greater scheme of things – a man of great courage and heart who cared for his fellow beings and made what little difference he could. He was a man of his time who tells us his story in the first person voice. He saw, thought, felt, believed what he experienced as it affected him and his country.

1

He was an American.

Illustrations

David Wexley in 1862

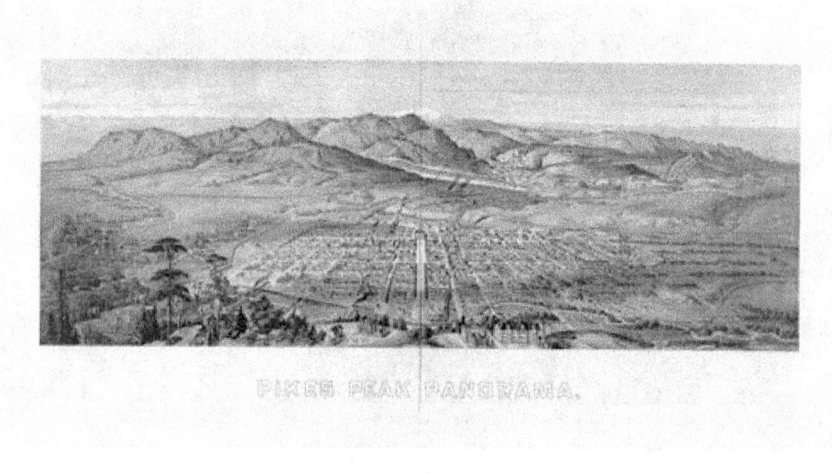

Map of the western United States in the late 19th century

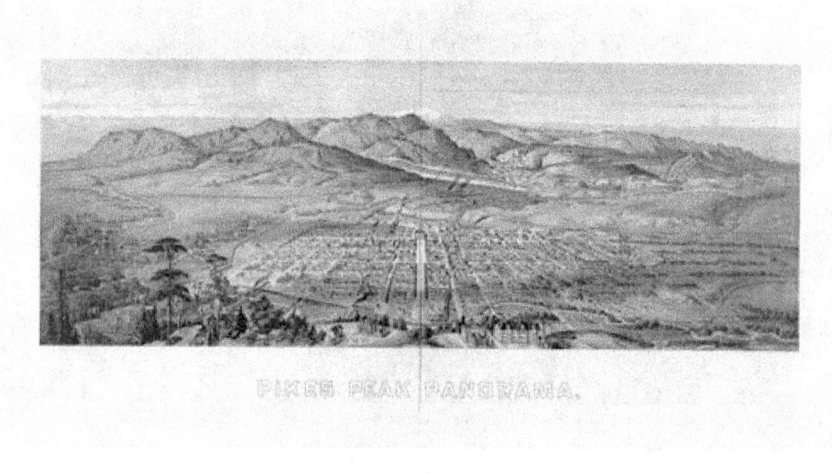

Pikes Peak in the Rocky Mountains

One – David

War is hell. War is never glorious. It don't matter what the cause, the purpose, the intent, or the outcome of it is. Human beings are killed. I know that because when I was a young man I seen it and participated in it. I killed human beings.

When I was a young boy in Baltimore, my life was comfortable. My widowed father Morgan had raised me in a fine house not far from the harbor. I was his only child. He was a successful banker, while he filled my mind with the things about history and politics he believed I needed to know. I neglected to mention my name is David Wexley.

But my young spirit was filled with youthful things. I wanted adventure. With his blessings, I left Baltimore's harbor at sixteen and headed to sea with the Merchant Marines. It was 1848 and in those days we still sailed in topsail schooners.

Those times I kept a journal of my travels. It was what we did the long lonely weeks out at sea and a good way to record my memories. Besides, I could share my stories with my father someday back home.

After a few years, I had grown up some and seen the American Atlantic coast at ports-of-call in Boston, Norfolk, Charleston and Savannah. I had learned something about the American people and what they valued in their lives as that differed from the North to the South. The beautiful coastal southern cities were charming. I fell for the southern gentility and elegance of the high-tone people there. Their lives were full of their traditional history, comfort and ease.

I was still so young then. There was no capacity of experience to draw from for me to understand, or even recognize, what was behind the façade of refinement. I would learn later what it meant and would ultimately lead to.

But genuine, salt-of-the-earth, hard-working people were in all those places too. I knew that even back then as young as I was. In any event, the life on the sea was out of my system. That was before the war.

When I returned to my father's house in Baltimore, I was ready for change and maybe new adventure. Following in the footsteps of a banker was not the life I wanted for me.

I wanted to build things, so I entered the carpentry trade as an apprentice. It was gratifying building new homes for Baltimore's people as I watched the city's growth begin to really boom. I enjoyed the comradery with my tradesmen in the long after-hours in the taverns after the day's hard work and began to understand the working-class men as I became one of them.

That is when Morgan began to teach me the grownup things he said I needed to know about the direction our country was headed. By then my travels and maturity had given me a sense of our history and my idealism was in full bloom.

We read the Maryland newspapers together and discussed the events as they were revealed and depicted by the conflicting viewpoints of the reporters and their editors. We talked about the abolitionists in the North and the slaveholders in the South and the

6

troubles in the West. The rift in the country between North and South would surely soon tear it apart. Decades of compromise had only prolonged the inevitable.

It had started as early as Adams and Jefferson. Washington had warned us in his kindly, affectionate way when he left office and wrote us his parting Farewell Address letter. He wanted us to be one nation with love for each other and our brand new country. He gently reminded us with his passionate, patriotic love to work together – east to west and north to south – and avoid factions and parties that might destroy us before very long. He had a good sense of the future.

For Adams and Jefferson had had two different visions for our country, while both loved our land and its new Constitution. Later Lincoln would see it as Washington had and tell us once more what we needed to do as a country and as moral human beings.

War would come soon and it was time to take sides. In Maryland both factions were present. The split often occurred in one family. My sense of morality, instilled from Morgan, was strong. I signed up for the Union with my best friend, the man who I worked for and had taught me the carpentry trade. He was Geoff Braxton from Baltimore and we signed up together.

Geoff and I met a man from Boston, Massachusetts who had signed up at the same time and joined us for our military training. The three of us became comrades in arms. We were going to fight for Burnside. We became close friends, the three amigos, spending our times in the taverns at night.

This was all brand new. It was going to be a great adventure. Our heads were full of visions of glory. We were so certain we would lick the rebels in short order. Everybody said the war couldn't last more than three months. It turned out the southerners were a hell of a lot tougher than anybody knew. We were so innocent of the reality that was to come.

I fought in two major battles in the Civil War. The first was near Sharpsburg in Maryland by Antietam Creek in '62. We repulsed Bobby Lee's first attempt at advance into the North and he had to retreat across the Potomac back into Virginia. The price we paid in lost lives was horrific. I came through it with sound body but lost one of my two friends there on the Burnside Bridge.

Late in '64 I fought my second battle in what they called the Battle of the Wilderness. We got caught in the swamp forest on our way to take Jeff Davis' Confederate capital at Richmond. The battle was a draw and General Grant disengaged. They had stopped us short of our goal. I was shot in the leg and the enemy who captured me thought I was a goner. I had lost so much blood. I woke up a prisoner in the Confederate hospital in Richmond.

They transported me to the Confederate prison at Andersonville and I suffered in that hell hole most of the last year of the war. There I found my other friend. He died of starvation and disease in my arms. The war changed me in so many ways I cannot tell you. I left my youthful idealism there in southwest Georgia. I was no longer that man of moral certainty, that man of innocence who knew just what must be done.

My wartime experiences are engraved in my memory and have permanently scarred my soul. I had learned a new master trade and, through my apprenticeship in battle, had learned the skills of how to kill and not be killed. My time in prison camp had showed me what it all came to, the heart-wrenching loss of friendship, the vindictive cruelty of the victors over the vanquished, the predatory behavior of our own comrades toward each other, the worst of humanity and the futility of war.

When I was released, I didn't want to go home. I missed my father but just could not. I had kept up my journal through the war, although not as faithfully as during my maritime adventures. Then I stopped. My last entry was made when I was walking across Alabama and met some poor plain folk who shared their ideas of faith with me. It was only then that I could write my father a letter explaining all that had happened in the battles, at Andersonville and the deaths of Geoff and Pat.

Inexplicably I was drawn to these people and their lives in the South. They were common but there was a nobility in their resilience, grit and unconquerable spirit. Much later in my life I would learn where it came from and why it compelled me.

I wandered west for many weeks on foot until I came to the Mississippi in Natchez. Beside the Big Muddy that afternoon, I met a man who would become my lifelong friend – my brother. But that is getting ahead of myself.

———————————◦———————————

After the war and on my own without my father, I made a study of the Civil War I had fought in, needing to understand it better. I studied the great men behind the scenes I had never known – men like Lincoln and Grant and Lee.

In the middle of the war, some twenty months since it began at Fort Sumter, President Lincoln was in trouble. He was struggling to preserve the Union up to that point. Emancipation of the slaves would come later. The war had come to a halt and a stalemate. Both sides were entrenched holding their gains and not moving forward.

Lincoln was beset with so many problems just then; he was alternately standing still, moving forward and making mistakes, and

9

constantly changing strategy trying to end it. His generals were pulling him in all directions. The American people of the Union were out of patience and despondent from the loss of blood and treasure and time. Even his Secretary of War said to him about a military appointment, "Well, you have made your choice of idiots. Now you can await the news of terrible disaster." They blamed it all on him.

His own Republicans in Congress, the Radical ones, and the newspapers were constantly harassing him, calling him an ignorant and incompetent fool. Even some members of his own cabinet were against him. But he persevered and spent his time thinking and writing. He believed he could convince them if he could just craft the most compelling words.

He had written a preliminary Emancipation Proclamation but his Secretary of State, William Seward advised him to put it in a drawer until the time was right. He taught Lincoln that timing was everything.

When he released it, the time was right. You might not believe this, but freeing the slaves was not its purpose. He had learned the skill of politics and the Proclamation would benefit him and the federal government fourfold.

First, it would not offend the tenuous relationship he held with the Union border-states – Delaware, Kentucky, Maryland and Missouri - who held slaves. They would be allowed to keep their slaves.

Second, it would not free slaves in the north – in the Union. He wanted to appease certain members of Congress. It only freed slaves in Union controlled Confederate states.

Third, he needed replenishment of troops by then and black freedmen could serve in the Union army. Runaways from the South and Border States were encouraged by his action and joined the army. Newly freed blacks in Confederate areas joined the Federals right on the spot when they came through. Lincoln was planning for this and knew what would happen.

In all arms, two million men fought in the Civil War. This was near the end and eighty thousand Negroes joined and fought bravely in cruel defeats like at Fort Wagner. Some, still slaves, served their Confederate masters in the war, digging, cooking, hauling, lifting and serving. Perhaps a handful did so willingly and believed in their cause.

Fourth, and not much known, he was constantly competing with Jeff Davis for foreign sympathy and support in England and France. They needed Jeff's cotton but hated his slavery. Lincoln hoped this would fool them and sway them to the Union side. It might not have been convincing to some overseas who saw through to its veiled purposes, but at least it kept them from swinging to Jeff Davis' side. Lincoln was walking a tightrope.

About that time, Lincoln came into his own. He had begun master-crafting those compelling words he needed. In his December message to Congress, a long fifty thousand words delivered by a moderator in his absence, it began with a blessing followed by well-wishing, a grieving about the war, and launched into a long host of boring humdrum matters. It was a dry beginning. After nearly losing them, it began to hit its stride at mid-point when the tone changed.

He wrote, "A nation may be said to consist of its territory, its people, and its laws. The territory is the only part which is of certain durability. 'One generation passeth away, and another generation cometh: but the earth abideth forever.' It is of the first importance to duly consider and estimate this ever-enduring part. That portion of the earth's surface which is owned and inhabited by the people of the United States is well adapted to be the home of one national

11

family, and it is not well adapted for two or more.... There is no line, straight or crooked, suitable for a national boundary upon which to divide. Trace through, from east to west, upon the line between the free and slave country, and we shall find a little more than one-third of its length are rivers, easy to be crossed and populated, or soon to be populated, thickly upon both sides; while nearly all its remaining lengths are merely surveyors' lines, over which people may walk back and forth without any consciousness of their presence."

What he was getting at and talking about here was his own native, interior, land-locked, region needing access to seacoasts and ports for the good of the nation.

He added further that, "Our national strife springs not from our permanent part, not from the land we inhabit, not from our national homestead.... Our strife pertains to ourselves – to the passing generations of men; and it can without convulsion be hushed forever with the passing of one generation."

This brought him at last to the heart of the matter in his mind when he wrote, "Without slavery the rebellion could never have existed; without slavery it could not continue."

His last words to the Congressmen on this occasion were, "..... The fiery trial through which we pass will light us down, in honor or dishonor, to the latest generation. We say we are for the Union. The world will not forget that we say this. We know how to save the Union. The world knows we do know how to save it. We – even we here – hold the power and bear the responsibility. In giving freedom to the slave, we assure freedom to the free – honorable alike in what we give and what we preserve. We shall nobly save or meanly lose the last, best hope of earth. Other means may succeed; this could not fail. The way is plain, peaceful, generous, just – a way which, if followed, the world will forever applaud, and God must forever bless."

12

The cost for what Mr. Lincoln was requesting was immeasurably great. Of course "we here" would not be able to do anything to assure anything. It would have to be done by young men who are farmers or teachers or merchants and follow old generals into battle.

Jeff Davis, as the President of the Confederacy, his country, had his own views and demons to deal with also. On the occasion that he came back home to Richmond on January 5, after an extensive, exhaustive trip to the west of his country and review of his Generals' performances, he just wanted to rest and be with his family. But the people were anxious to see him, grateful for his return and wanted to celebrate his appearance.

And so he mustered up the energy from his meager reserves, was invigorated by the people and spoke to them. He told them: "Every sound is the voice of my child and every child renews the memory of a loved one's appearance, but none can equal their charms, nor can any compare with my own long-worshipped Winnie", he had written home from Tennessee but believed he could not ignore the adoration from the crowd of his people and the courtesy they tendered.

"I am happy to be welcomed on my return to the capitol of the Confederacy – the last hope, as I believe, for the perpetuation of that system of government which our forefathers founded – the asylum of the oppressed, and the home of true representative liberty."

With his strained and exhausted voice which usually gathered in strength when he continued, he reverted to the deeds of olden days in the Old Dominion, where the earlier Revolution had been proclaimed, begun, and finally won. And so now he told these new Virginians, "anticipating the overthrow of that government which you had inherited, you assumed to yourselves the right, as your fathers had done before you, to declare yourself independent, and nobly have you advocated the assertion which you have made. Here,

13

upon your soil, some of the fiercest battles of the Revolution were fought, and upon your soil it closed by the surrender of Cornwallis. Here again our men of every state; here they have congregated, linked in the defense of a most sacred cause. They have battled, they have bled upon your soil, and it is now consecrated by blood which cries for vengeance against the insensate foe of religion as well as of humanity, of the altar as well as of the hearthstone.

It is true, you have a cause which binds you together more firmly than your fathers were. They fought to be free from the usurpations of the British crown, but they fought against a manly foe. You fight against the off-scourings of the earth.

Every crime which could characterize the course of demons has marked the course of the invader ... from the burning of defenseless towns to the stealing of silver forks and spoons."

Whether the price for that war was worth it is incalculable. After all I have seen on the ground, it pains me to consider it glory. I still believe it is right, but there is no glory. No glory whatsoever.

The commanding officers talked about glory. They were doing their job – what they were trained to do – getting us to march, to entrench, to stand up to withering fire from artillery and muskets, to charge with clashing bayonets, to staunch the bleeding, to bury the dead. There is no glory, just aggression meeting aggression.

Some called us killer angels. I never saw it that way. It may be honor. I do not know. It is not noble. Josiah tried to help me understand it and bring me peace through his God. I am not a Godly man.

I met Josiah Ashford, a just-freed slave, at the dockside of the Mississippi at Natchez. He had walked the fifteen miles over there from his former plantation, Savannah Oaks nearby that same day he had been freed. I had walked for many days from Andersonville in Georgia. We talked as strangers and became friends. I went with him all over Mississippi and Alabama looking for his lost wife taken from him. We set our fortunes together.

When we found she had been killed on another plantation, we had an altercation. I shot and killed the overseer. We stole two horses and headed north. He was a master cabinetmaker who made furniture. I was a master carpenter who built buildings. As I said, he became my brother.

Two – Ohio

Josiah and I finally found our way to Hamilton, Ohio late in '65. We had made our way north on horseback, the one's we stole in Alabama, up the Tennessee and along the Ohio to Cincinnati. Hamilton is just north of Cincinnati and it seemed like the right place to stop and figure out what to do.

When Joe had learned that he had a lost daughter from his killed wife Josena, he was doubly heartbroken we couldn't find her. So we decided to give up on the South and head north. He consoled me when we visited Shiloh and I consoled him for his great personal losses also. The war had cost us both plenty.

We did carpentry jobs for the farmers and town folks until we had enough money for Josiah to buy a small farm. He had no intention of being a farmer. Joe wanted to start a furniture making business. I stayed with him and we renovated the old barn to begin his humble factory. Before you knew it, we had been there for years and I guess it was home.

Joe made beautiful furniture and soon established a reputation for his work. His business took off and very quickly he was selling his fine furniture to farmers and town folk all over southwestern Ohio. I helped him build a proper factory in place of the renovated old barn.

I was always inventive with my work once I had developed the skills with my tools and hands. Starting back in Ohio with Joe's factory, I had begun to think like an engineer or an architect. To do it, it needs you to visualize and then build it the way you see it in your mind. It is the same with carpentry or machinery.

He met a fine woman, Mary Custis, whose people had come there years ago from Virginia. She was a 4th generation freeborn Negro from Martha Curtis Washington's slaves. They married and had twins. The girl was named Josena after his first wife who was killed. The boy was named David after me. I was honored and stayed close to the growing family as the twins grew up.

Joe was so popular, he got elected to the Ohio legislature up in Columbus. He spent time up there when they were in session. I was so proud of how far my friend had come since I found him in Natchez as a newly freed slave all those years ago.

Back in Ohio, Joe developed an extensive library. His might have been bigger than my father Morgan's. Once Joe learned to read, his intellect and knowledge on all manner of things grew at an incredible rate. We had many discussions our years together. Sure, I taught him some history, but he taught me philosophy and law. We both were concerned about the direction of the country. That's where all these subjects came together. We both wanted the common man, be he Negro or poor white, to have an equal chance for a fair share if he worked for it. Joe's special interest was for the next generations of Negroes to get a good education.

For me, I stayed in town and ran a small carpentry business. It kept me busy building new houses and repairing old buildings for the area which was growing fast. I eventually hired two men to help me. I was getting a little older and it was good to have a couple young bucks to help with the heavy lifting.

I had my one chance for a wife and love of my life, but it didn't work out. Jim Culpepper wouldn't stand for me marrying his daughter Estelle. She was a colored woman and me marrying her was taboo in those days. It broke my heart and I went back to drinkin'.

Joe tried to get me through it, but after a while, I decided to start over. I still reflect on my lost youth and innocence.

I remember Estelle while I think about our fight for the freedom of colored people. After so many years living in Ohio, I just didn't seem to notice color anymore. I was very attracted to some colored women the same as any other shade of skin. It was such a liberating feeling compared to all the preconceptions and feelings everybody had back in Baltimore before the war.

After Lincoln was killed, that son-of-a-bitch Andrew Johnson took over and messed up most of what so many of us had fought and died for. Lincoln never would have picked him as his Vice President. His own Republican party did that even though Johnson was a Democrat from Tennessee of suspicious southern sympathies. The war still kept going, but now we were fighting it in our minds.

When General Grant picked up the reins, I think he did a fair job. He was a man from Point Pleasant, Ohio you know. He was born there along the Ohio River in 1822, not more than fifty five miles from where me and Josiah settled in Hamilton in 1865.

Everyone said he was a failure at everything in his life with the exception of his military career. They said he was a lousy President and administrator and couldn't resolve the scandal of the spoils system rampant all about him.

That may be true to some degree but I know his heart and it was certainly more genuine than McClellan or Sheridan or Sherman. At least President Grant tried to finish up what the war was for – he understood it – and improve the country by mitigating the many hateful actions in the South and selfish political nonsense in Washington.

But he sent the red headed Ohioan Sherman – his old friend and colleague who he had spent so much time talking to and strategizing and commiserating with, smoking cigars, while the newspapers called one a drunk and the other a lunatic - out west to kill Indians. Sherman stayed there and managed that for 15 years.

It was sort of like the time long before when General Andrew Jackson was President and did the same to the American native peoples back in the East.

As far as politics go, I still try to steer clear of it as much as I can. Unlike my father, I don't enjoy debating it or the party factions. But like him, I think historically as the best means to understand the present state of affairs. I guess I am a Jacksonian Democrat, the founder of that new view of democracy. Old Hickory did some despicable things at the beginning of this century that are shameful to our history. He was an Indian killer, a slaveholder and a self-made wealthy man who challenged the eastern elites. He believed strongly in States rights and acted to close down the national bank.

But he was a rugged frontiersman and a Scots-Irish fighter. Like me, he believed in the common man. Nobody is my superior and I am free to live my own life as I please within the limits of the law.

President Grant made William T. Sherman the Commanding General of the Army which Cump was from 1869 to 1883. That's all Cump ever wanted to be. He had said he would never stand for political office under any circumstance and I respected him for that.

All Sherman knew was that war was hell and he knew how to fight it. He just wanted to follow orders and use his genius for the invention of modern warfare. It was for him the Esprit de Corps – all he ever wanted to have, be and do. When he died years later in 1891 – a few years after I left for the West - he had lived in New York City and they held his funeral there. Confederate General Joe Johnston came and served his former enemy as his pallbearer.

For these men it was always about the Esprit de Corps. I was just a lowly foot soldier and most often despised the senior officers and thought them heartless and incompetent. We all did. But I understand their Esprit de Corps and dedication.

Then President Hayes oversaw the end of Reconstruction, after Grant did what he could, and tried to reconcile the divisions still in the country. Now it is Benjamin Harrison in 1891. Who knows what he will be, stand for or do? While I respect some men, I hate politics as a general proposition. There have been so many disappointments in the past and there will be again in the future.

Three – The Trip

———————⊃o⊂———————

I always like to travel light. Other than the practical convenience of that, I think the measure of a man's character is not how he acts when he has everything, but how he acts when he has nothing.

Does he jealously covet what the other man has? Or does he wish him well when he has more? With less, a man is freer. With more it is a burden worrying about losing all you have. All I need is a good horse, a rifle and a blanket roll.

That is not exactly true. When I left I carried a gunny sack with two clean shirts, some socks and a toothbrush. These were modern, more civilized times. But my blanket roll was like my old friend I had carried all over my travels in the South. And of course I carried my Army Colt.

It has been decades since I had rode the train. Back in '64, I rode the Confederate prison train from Richmond to Andersonville and swore that would be my last. But I knew that this trip was impractical to attempt on horseback. The railroad was the only way to do it.

The trains had been around the East a long time and were an important part of the war. For me though, the trip out West would be a new adventure.

From Cincinnati, the Baltimore and Ohio line went east which was no good. There was a local line between Cincinnati, Lebanon and Dayton, but that wouldn't get me very far. I figured I needed to find some way to Chicago. It was a major crossroads from the East to the West with all the cattle, slaughterhouses and meatpacking going on there. From there I could easily go west out to St. Louis or Kansas City or places in Wyoming, Montana or Colorado – most anywhere I wanted.

Josiah told me I couldn't get there from Cincinnati, nearby where we lived in the village of Ashford, in the town of Hamilton. So he offered to give me a ride in his buggy carriage northeast up to Columbus. I agreed to this, his last kindness, and he followed his familiar route up to Columbus, the capital where his legislature was.

He came into the train station and stood by me while I bought my ticket. We sat outside on a bench quietly watching the tracks, waiting for the train. After a while we saw it coming up the track going west, almost right on time. We stood up and faced each other in silence.

Joe looked at me with sad eyes brimming over with tears, that face forever full of resolve and said "I will never forget you. We have shared together so much of our lives. I will think of you always. God speed and be well my brother."

I felt inside that same sadness he showed on his face and told him you know me better than anyone in my life. You know I have to go. I will think about you and wish you were with me for all the new things I will discover and do. You are the best friend I have ever known and I will miss you the rest of my days.

We clasped forearms in the old Roman way as men do that have great respect, admiration and affection for one another. We stood facing each another moment and I began to turn away as the conductor called "All aboard." I walked a few steps and turned back once again looking at the man I had loved and respected for so long.

———————————◦————————————

Later, after we were apart for some years, I thought about Joe and our long time together. It was true what he said. He always spoke truth to me. My friend Joe was only three years older than me and came from a lowly place as a slave. But in many ways he was like my father Morgan, steering me toward a better and safer path.

I had left him my old journals to keep, thinking they might mean something to him as a keepsake to remember me. Maybe his wife Mary would enjoy reading about those olden times long ago in my youth. Maybe his grown children David and Josena would want to read about their Uncle David. With a sadness in his eyes, Joe humbly accepted them.

Now I have no further interest in keeping them. There is no need. I have no family or kin. The rest of my life, I will learn how to live in the moment. Whatever tomorrow brings, I will be there to see.

Joe cared for me and saw when my adventuresome spirit got too risky and close to danger. It could be self-destructive. He saw that and I knew it too. I couldn't help but notice that Joe could see it. He found ways to stay out of trouble and work with troublesome people and it made him happy. I just couldn't and never have been happy.

He was my safe harbor, like the lighthouse showing me the way out of troubled waters. It reminds me of storms on the Atlantic when I was a young Merchant Marine.

But I couldn't follow his beacon, any more than I could my father's, and kept looking for new ways to get into trouble, not really on purpose, not consciously, but true all the same. Trouble always found itself in front of my road and I couldn't or wouldn't walk around it.

It was true the last words I said to him and I never forgot them. I really missed him and wished he had been here with me these times. But that is my fault, not his. I had to leave him for whatever it is that drives me onto the next thing.

He was the older brother I never had. I will always love that man. He told me we would be together again someday in this life or the next. I sure hope he was right.

The Columbus Chicago and Indiana railroad was there. It had been leased to the Pennsylvania railroad since 1869. It went right from Columbus to Chicago, stopping to transfer in Fort Wayne.

Chicago in 1887 was a peculiar mix of wealth and squalor. I never cared for either of those things about cities. That's why I preferred steering clear of them as much as I could. The new local electric streetcars and elevated railway systems joined together with steam railroads making it easy to get around and in and out of that steaming mass of humanity. Doubting I would ever see this place again, I decided to stay for a short while and explore the city.

Even though I am put off by the crowds and squalor in big cities, I couldn't help but admire the architecture in the Windy City. It is the fastest growing city in the United States. It was a wonder to see the way they are planning and rebuilding the core of the city, after the fire in 1871, inside the beautiful river loop that comes in from Lake Michigan on the east and curves south. The arched stone bridges rising up and over to cross that pretty river were impressive.

Folks told me they are planning to build grand hotels along Michigan Avenue. State Street is booming with new life. Beautiful municipal parks are being planned and built along the great lake, starting with the new Lincoln Park. They have big plans and dreams I can appreciate. It was plenty worth it to see it all for a couple days.

But the heartbeat of the city is not its new architecture emerging from the aftermath of the fire. It is the Union Stockyards, the South Work steel mills and the Pullman railway-car plant. These are the places where the people work, where things get built, where dreams are turned into reality.

Before long, I naturally gravitated to the working class people and their neighborhoods. In a big city these are the darkest, filthiest and most crowded streets with tenements packing people densely together.

Their gathering places are the saloons – the centers of their working poor communities. They are served friendship and comradery there, just as I had known in Baltimore a life ago. These are the workingman's clubs, their trade union halls and guilds. The patrons look out for each other, discuss politics, and assist each other in finding employment – a working man school for both the working man scholar and the working man teacher. The saloons are the common ethnic ground without the shame of charity or the outside rules and restrictions of organized clubs. I felt at home.

(David would never know it, but just a few years later Josena and David Ashford would visit the magnificent Chicago World's Fair and Columbian Exposition in 1893 as wide-eyed young adults just after graduating from Oberlin College.

And in 1900, the year he was killed, progressive temperance reformers believing that saloons seduced customers into lives of drunkenness, crime and debauchery, studied them to find solutions to the perceived problems. Prominent sociologist Royal Melendy began a serious academic study of this social problem with this same premise. He learned that he was wrong and that saloons served their communities better than any institution available at the time. Reluctantly, he reported his findings to the doubting intelligentsia of his time.

Melendy had an opportunity for a further life lesson learned if he took it; that is to never accept the premise on the face of it from your opponent or anyone for that matter. If you do, it will lead you unavoidably to their conclusion.)

—————————————⇒◦⇐—————————————

From Chicago there was railroads going every which way, to anyplace you wanted to go to by the late 1800's. There was a funny disconnect though back by the Mississippi. East of the Big Muddy there was railroads everywhere and for a long time, like I have told you. The West had railroads too. What was needed was better connections across the big river in the northern continentals and the southern ones as well.

Actually the term transcontinental railroad is misleading. They weren't one continuous road like it sounds. They were many separate links joined together sometimes in a roughshod manner.

While we traveled on the train the few days to Denver, I watched out the window at the rapidly passing scene as the land changed in its shape, color, and texture. The landscape from the Midwest to the West, across the prairies to the mountains, took on a moving panorama of diverse beauty. I couldn't help but be moved by how great and vast was our land – America. It was so new, so sparsely populated; almost still pristine in its breathtaking, awe inspiring barrenness.

The Mississippi River is on the west side of Illinois and forms the boundary with the next state west – Iowa. Chicago is on the east side of Illinois along the shore of Lake Michigan. So the railroads heading west of Chicago are all confronted by the challenge of getting across the Mississippi. That Big Muddy, the Mississippi Delta, makes me think about the Nile in Egypt – all that rich silt piling up and creating a vast area of fertility.

As we crossed that great river on a new railroad bridge, I remembered Lincoln's words – what he said about our enduring land and its rivers dividing it and that they were soon to be crossed. So the division was a temporary thing and we the people of this nation would conquer that too. I hoped this would portend greater things for our people as a symbol or omen of unity.

I was traveling in relative comfort, in a peaceful time with friendly, forward-looking hopeful people. It was so completely different and positive than my ride decades ago in the prison train from Richmond to Andersonville. The people traveling with me on the trip were just regular people – maybe teachers or engineers or hopeful businessmen – but with enough means to take the train.

The very poor, maybe alone or with families, couldn't afford this modern, comfortable, fast way to get across the country. They had to come in wagons with all their meager possessions and face the hardships and dangers to make their way that I didn't. I had saved some money and I felt lucky even sitting on these hard seats and eating cold sandwiches for many long days.

Oh, I know there are a few back there in freight cars taking their chances the conductor or porters won't catch them. They have only the food and water they can carry until they hop off when they get where they want to go.

And there are the rich in the private cars with sleeping berths and fine dining surrounded by mahogany and brass appointed accommodations like a moving mansion or palace.

Still I'm fortunate I have the means to travel like I do. I do prefer to keep my own company and avoid crowds and numbers of people herded together like cattle in any case. But despite all the layovers and inefficiencies, I'll be on the other side of the country real quick. In the meantime, I have seen the new towns springing up along the path of the railroads and the development across all the places in this American century.

West of the river, there was railroads springing up like crazy and catching up fast to the East. But railroads crossing that river boundary made for some difficulties and covered strange geographical directions and peculiarities that were inconvenient and not very sensible.

For my time here in the American country, they called it the Gilded Age and the railroads were at the heart of the country's social and economic history. It was full of corruption from the managers of the big railroad companies and their partnership with government.

This was the time when we started to use the word corporations and that word was synonymous with railroads. So the Gilded Age had more to do with wealth gained from rotten means than it did about finding gold.

We built the western railroads faster than we needed them and they failed as businesses one after another while their leaders and planners and money managers got rich. It was about operating on credit with government, not about profit and success, and walking away with other people's money when the companies went bust.

I think the Gilded Age is so much about the railroads. The greed, corruption and shenanigans we learn about were all about the railroads in one way or another. Like the Civil War itself, the railroads brought some good and some bad to my country, but at a great price.

There were reformers who constantly tried to rein in the power of the railroads. That power as always was about what some men did to others, not about the locomotives, equipment or tracks.

The railroad men had power that reached out to so many aspects of our economy and men's lives. They could extort favor from a community to run their rails close by to it or bypass the community and place their rails far away to cause one community to wither and another to grow. America had never seen anything like it before.

For me it wasn't anything I could do about it. I just see it and know what is happening.

The railroad companies competed with other business activities and with themselves as well. They lobbied the government and curried favor to pass regulations to hurt the competition and favor themselves. In a perverse way they were part of the reform themselves.

That Economic Panic of 1893 was caused by the railroad men and their corporations and the relationships they formed as groups of friends with our government. It was because they wanted to develop our country out here in the West at all costs. The waste of money, treatment of native peoples and foreigners (new immigrants) was all part of that driving American motivation – our self-belief in Manifest Destiny. The development did come but again, like my war, the cost to human lives was horrific.

Most of the railroad buildin' was done by 1890 for the West. The sound and the fury of it was in the 60's, 70's and 80's. But the economic and physical damage to some Americans would take a bit longer to end.

Anyway, The Union Pacific headed west from Chicago to Cheyenne, Wyoming, stopping for transfer. Then another leg, already part of the Union Pacific, continued to Ft. Collins in Colorado and due south on to Denver City.

While we slept in our seats at night, we stopped at the changeovers and got off the train a while to stretch our legs. Standing still once in a while for a brief time, we got to see the towns as places fixed in their positions. This was another perspective.

I talked with some of my fellow travelers on the many long legs of the trip, but most were lost in their private thoughts or taking all the time to read their books. I did get to read Mark Twain's *The Gilded Age*, first published in 1873, about what was happening in the country.

One lady sitting next to me saw me reading it and struck up a conversation with me. She asked me what I thought about Twain's condemnation of the western railroad industry and our government's participation in the crime. I told her he wrote it like it is with his own unique brand of humor about American life.

She was coming west from Virginia. I told her I was from Maryland and knew the East – the North and South of it – but had never been west of Ohio, let alone Chicago and parts west of the Mississippi.

People were going west to seek a new life for all kinds of reasons. There were even some mail-order brides. What a desperate thing that seemed like, but who am I to know or to judge?

One woman I spoke with was planning to go out to the prairie near Topeka, Kansas and open up a schoolhouse. She had been offered a position as a teacher by the townsfolk there. Somehow they had sought her out and she decided to pick up from Massachusetts and do it. I could not but wonder how brave and dedicated she must be to strike off alone into the unknown and certainly face the hardship and deprivation that would surely come to her. Her true grit was admirable. Other courageous and dedicated women like her have helped build this country.

When I finally arrived in Denver, I found it was a crazy western town. It ended up for reasons that happened later, I stayed there for quite a long time.

The city was growing up and down and sideways, hectic with new people rushing around and anxious to hit the hills for gold or silver. Usually it has a very dry high-desert climate, but occasionally flash floods or more often the spring melt-off, drown it in water and mud. When I got there, the streets were ankle deep in mud and the sidewalks were covered with wooden board planking to dry off muddy boots. There were far more saloons than churches. I don't think I saw a church.

I knew soon as I got there I would need a horse. Just like the old days with Joe in the South, it was the only way to get around. We had kept them up in Ohio too. We loved them for the fine partners they were. I found me that good horse. The way that it happened was this.

In Denver City, I met a fine young woman, too young for me, name of Darcy Farrow in a saloon in town. She was friendly and we got to talking. After some moments, we moved from the bar to a table off to the side and shared some whisky and talk. After some whiskey, we got mellow and the talk turned sentimental.

Darcy was a wonder to see. Her voice was the sweetest ever to land on my ear. Her eyes shone like bright lights. She had this way of touching my arm when we talked close. Her touch was as soft as a feather. I could tell right from the first, when I brought it up, she was a horsewoman.

She was a Scot like me. It surprised me how many came out West as pioneers. Mostly I thought they had settled down the spine of the Appalachians and into the South, with a few up into the remote areas of Maine. But we have an adventuresome spirit, so it makes sense how many had come out here.

She came from the Carson Valley Plain, from Yerington near Carson City, Nevada. The Walker River runs by there. It's fed from Sierra Nevada snowmelt and empties to the south in Walker Lake.

She told me all her stories about that territory. It had become a new state in 1868. There its people were mining for gold and silver before this new rush to Colorado for silver. Just after the war a lot happened out there that had begun well before it. Silver mined from Virginia City helped finance and may have saved the Union. It was known all over the country in the 19th century for its mining boom.

Carson City, Nevada, named after Kit Carson, was over on the eastern edge of the Sierra Nevada. The Virginia and Truckee Railroad ran from there in 1864. The railroad was named after Virginia City and the Truckee River. Nearby Yerington, Nevada was named after Henry M. Yerington, Superintendent of the Truckee Railroad since 1868. The Truckee carried a lot of bullion from the rural highlands of Virginia City to Carson City. Mark Twain reported news about it later in 1868 as reminiscence of his journalism career there in Nevada.

Darcy knew horses and she loved to talk about them. She was looking for something better just like I was. Like I told you, saloons are the places where folks come together to meet, talk, drink, gamble, dance and maybe fall in love. Sometimes they are the places where people argue and get into a fight, but not usually. Usually it is a place of relaxation and community.

She had moved to Denver City just four years ago after her betrothed jilted her. I cannot imagine how that could have happened.

When we got ready to leave and walked out, I saw she had a limp in her leg like me. She said her pony stumbled and fell on her a few years back and she felt lucky to have survived it. I told her I did too with my war wounds and time in the prison camp in Georgia.

Out on the boardwalk in front of the saloon, we paused a few moments to say goodbye. She knew I had been looking for a good horse to travel west, so she suggested I go see the McAuley ranch just outside town toward the west. She pointed me in that direction even though we were both lookin' that way at the sunset.

We gave each other a long embrace. That was the last time I ever saw Darcy Farrow for a dozen years. She was always on my mind for all that time.

To be honest about our self-view of resolute strength, there is an opposite side too. Probably from the Irish, it is a sad melancholy fatalism. In moments of weakness, when our guard is down, we don't always believe everything will work out for the best.

But we draw from this sadness, this fatalistic romanticism, also as a source of our strength. It flows out of us in our poetry, often released with our whiskey.

Four – The Gilded Age

While I saw changes and development in my country after the Civil War, I was aware of the parallel changes in the world in the late 19th century. We called it the Gilded Age sardonically with a taste of bitterness. Certainly, as its name implies, it was about getting rich - getting rich quick if you could. Much of our development was about thievery from investors going on between the railroad corporations and their friendly allies in government to accomplish that end.

In England it was the Victorian Age. Queen Victoria's reign from 1836 to the end of the century brought a new Renaissance of elegance and a blend of old world style with modern conveniences as the industrial world began to bloom in full. This was certainly not the first time this change came, but merely another cycle and a higher iteration of science, engineering, comfort and ease.

In my country, America it meant that the affluent adopted an affected ornate and elegant style of living and its trappings in their fine homes, including their furniture and decorations. Some would say it was over-decorated with every wall plastered with expensive paintings on a backdrop of vivid colored paint or deeply finished premium wood paneling, every fancy table or breakfront, in fact every horizontal surface, covered with coveted curios collected from exotic places. It was pretentious bragging if ever I have seen it.

It was big and dark while warmly lit with gas lamps and emerging electric lighting. Deep plush velvet, reds and browns, dominated the feel of the homes of the wealthy and those that could afford its pretense. It was an opulence fabricated to showcase the arrival of the successful.

It may have begun in London, but we saw it in Boston and New York and the French influence of it right down to the whorehouses in New Orleans and even out in the West. The extravagant excessiveness of it was apparent on the special railroad cars, ornately outfitted and well serving to the nouveau riche as they were conveyed west in the extreme of comfort.

I saw it emerging in Chicago and Denver City. There were pockets of such people and places in the midst of the dust, desolation and deprivation of the western desert and its settlers. There it was the land grabs, the cattle barons and the railroad barons.

The outward visible ostentatious opulence of the rich was offensive to me. I knew where they had got it, who earned it for them and who they stole it from.

On the surface of it, it was an age of grace and graciousness just like the Antebellum South was for its aristocratic planters and city merchants who factored cotton. But it was neither of these things in the truest senses. It was neither God's grace of benevolent love and protection, nor man's courtliness, manners or kindhearted care for his fellow being.

My early life in Baltimore with my father Morgan was comfortable and upper-middle class. It was not pretentious, just at ease for want of nothing. I have nothing against him. He was honest and never stole from anyone.

But my ideas of ease were not like his. I never wanted ease; I wanted adventure. I started that life as early as sixteen and never turned back. It led to working and living with the working class people, the common people and sometimes the poor. That was where I was felt comfortable and where I fit in. That was where I was at ease.

Five – Fannie

I hitched over there and met Fannie McAuley. She was alone with no sign of a man there at the ranch house. She greeted me friendly and we talked for hours. She did most of the talking and finally she showed me her horses.

She had come from Scotland, near the Borders in the lowlands, to Kentucky just at the end of the war. Her husband Angus and her settled in there to raise horses. Funny thing though, they had been Reivers and horse thieves back in the homeland, yet they came to raise horses in America legitimately.

So they learned how to raise Kentucky thoroughbreds on their land, in their new country. But the troubles and the turmoils there in Kentucky from the war were too much. They picked up and moved to Colorado. Here they learned to crossbreed thoroughbreds with western mustangs.

Fannie looked at me sincerely and told me none of that war meant anything to Angus and me. We didn't grow tobacco, or rice, or cotton, or sugar cane in Kentucky; we raised fine horses. We owned no slaves. We didn't appreciate Grant's or Sherman's Army of the Tennessee, or Morgan's Raiders from the Confederacy either.

Like all Scots, we just wanted to be left alone on our land and not see it destroyed by outsiders. We had no great army to protect ourselves, so we moved west. Even fighting Scots can recognize when a fight is not worth it. You may know our history and that we are the most feared in battle but this was not our fight.

If we had not moved quick, soldiers would have stolen our thoroughbreds and used them to haul caissons for cannon or supply wagons, starved them or blown them up in battles. That we could not abide. They would have to get their horses and mules elsewhere.

When they came there, just like back in Kentucky, Fannie and Angus McAuley together were a formidable force to be reckoned with. On her own now, Fannie was still a fierce, strong personality to deal with as well.

It ended up I stayed with Fannie. Angus had died a couple years ago when his heart gave out. We kept company and I helped her arrange her bed. Like every Scot, this Lassie, actually an older strong Scotswoman, couldn't pass up something for free, especially if a good bargain was struck for the benefit of the giver and the receiver. She was hard-bitten, hard-scrabble, but with mirth and satirical.

We spent our time together living in the moment. We didn't care what tomorrow might bring. It is poetic but true to a man's heart in love that while today the blossoms still clung to the vine, I tasted her strawberries. I drank her sweet wine. A million tomorrows may pass away, but I'll not forget the joy that was mine those days. She knew I was a rover, discontented with yesterday's glory and who I am from the song that I sang. Today was our moment. Come to bed she had said. We laughed and we cried and we sang. We had a powerful and poignant two seasons together.

I hadn't planned to, but I decided to stay a while with Fannie. Delaying my idea to get to Aspen, I thought this might be home. After all, this might have been what I have been seeking all the years since the war.

Fannie was younger than me and had no children. I had grown up without a mother but had always been fond of women. There was something going on here beneath the surface and beyond our recognition. She was always teaching me things – things about me my father never did. She intuited things about me. It was like nurturing in a way but not exactly like that. I found it sensually

38

attractive. She was a plain woman compared to some, but pretty enough. I was drawn in in a way I had never felt before.

Although I was older than she, it was sort of a mothering she gave me. She was a comfort I had never known. Come lay beside me and just rest your weary bones she would say on more than one occasion. Fold me in your arms and rest your troubled old head on my bosom lad and let the troubles of the world melt away.

As I lay enfolded in Fannie's arms, I cried for all the years of war I had seen and for the guilt and pain and loss I had carried for such a long time. It was a forgiveness for what I had done and a release from the tortured memories. I forgave myself for having survived it when so many thousands had not, so many lives cut short in their youth, lying dead still, torn apart on the fields the last I saw them and have been dreaming about them just as they were only a moment ago.

She got up and picked up a small book from her shelf above her davenport desk in the parlor. She walked back over toward me extending it forward in two hands, as though making an offering, her azure eyes smiling sadly, glistening with emotional sympathy. She sat back down on the sofa next to me, so close I felt her warmth.

This old book has poems in it I have enjoyed and that helped me get through the loss of Angus, she said. I want to read you selected parts of one by Wordsworth that deeply affected me and I have read it many, many times. It is about immortality and recollections of early childhood. I want you to know it.

Enfolded in Fannie's arms, she read me the parts that were important:

There was a time when meadow, grove, and stream,
The earth, and every common sight,
To me did seem
Apparelled in celestial light,

The glory and the freshness of a dream.
It is not now as it hath been of yore
Turn wheresoe'er I may,
By night or day.
The things which I have seen I now can see no more.

The Rainbow comes and goes,
And lovely is the Rose,
The Moon doth with delight
Look round her when the heavens are bare,
Waters on a starry night
Are beautiful and fair;
The sunshine is a glorious birth;
But yet I know, where'er I go,
That there hath past away a glory from the earth.

But there's a Tree, of many, one,
A single field which I have looked upon,
Both of them speak of something that is gone;
The Pansy at my feet
Doth the same tale repeat:
Whither is fled the visionary gleam?
Where is it now, the glory and the dream?

Our noisy years seem moments in the being
Of the eternal Silence: truths that wake,
To perish never;
Which neither listlessness, nor mad endeavour,
Nor Man nor Boy,
Nor all that is at enmity with joy,
Can utterly abolish or destroy!
Hence in a season of calm weather
Though inland far we be,
Our Souls have sight of that immortal sea
Which brought us hither,
Can in a moment travel thither,

And see the Children sport upon the shore,
And hear the mighty waters rolling evermore.

Thanks to the human heart by which we live,
Thanks to its tenderness, its joys, and fears,
To me the meanest flower that blows can give
Thoughts that do often lie too deep for tears.

We are not alone, no matter whatever our trials, disappointments or horrors. We are born with an unburdened soul – pure and immortal – able to see God's glory all around us in everything in nature and the world we behold. As we live life our soul becomes burdened and we cannot see His glory as we once could. It is difficult to put down our burden and be as authentic as we were born.

Enfolded in Fannie's arms, I told her I see the graves and worse still the dead unburied. The souls gone and untarnished have left behind the earthly pain. All the sorrows have been shed. Only those who still live shall carry it until it is our time.

Enfolded in Fannie's arms, she told me that all had found peace after they gave their last full measure of devotion and I must also.

After all these years, let us say the words that we were taught David. It is for them David, for their immortal souls and for ours. Say them with me:

Our Father which art in heaven,
Hallowed be thy name.
Thy Kingdom come.
Thy will be done in earth, as it is in heaven.
Give us our daily bread.
And forgive us our debts, as we forgive our debtors.
And lead us not into temptation, but deliver us from evil:
For thine is the kingdom, and the power, and the glory, for ever.

Amen

Enfolded in Fannie's arms, she told me it is goodness, light illuminating the darkness. It is the way out of our troubles. We are not alone.

This hard woman, so strong resilient and wise, she was the one who gave me the gift of peace of mind. It was a great dark thing had gone. We lay quietly together and looked into each other's eyes. It was peaceful. I slept better than I had in many years.

While she lived alone since Angus had died, she did have two young hands come in through the week to tend to the horses and do some general handiwork needed at the ranch.

Fannie's best hand Mike had designs on her which I could tell by the way he looked at her when she wasn't watching. After Mike saw what was happening between me and her, he kept to himself. There were never any hard feelings between me and Mike.

She told me Angus had taught her to load and shoot a double-barrel shotgun and a repeater Winchester rifle. They had coyotes, and sometimes a wolf or a bear coming down from the mountains, pesterin' their horses. She had got pretty good with long guns but she had not used a revolver.

Turns out she did have to fend off a couple raiders in the past with her long guns. They were two old Confederates from Quantrill's men from over in Missouri who had lived out their lives as bandits and desperados. Some men never learned how or when to stop the selfish takin' from others, or the dishonor in killing of innocents, after the war.

So we practiced and I taught her what I could about how to hold it steady and squeeze the trigger, not pull it. She would need to get used to the kick. Then I worked with her on gettin' faster, figurin' a hand gun would usually be needed if troublesome men showed up when I wasn't around.

We practiced with my Colt at first. We shot bottles off the top of fence posts at about thirty feet and she got better with practice. Fannie got pretty good at it after a while once she got used to it.

Then we went to town and I bought her a Colt 44 six gun. She knew I was thinking of her since someday I might be leavin'.

One time we were shootin' bottles out on the back lot when out of nowhere Fannie told me she loves the name David. It is heroic she said. It reminds me of the Valley of Elah. In the bible, there is the story of the great battle fought there between the Israelites and the Philistines. Goliath was the champion of the Philistines and a fearsome giant. David was a young boy who offered to the Israelite King Saul to go fight him. David faced Goliath without armor, just his staff, a sling and some stones from a brook.

Without fear he launched a stone from his sling which hit Goliath in the temple and smote him dead right there in his tracks. Surely the Lord was standing by David's side. David cut off Goliath's head and took it to Jerusalem to show the people. He grew up to become Israel's greatest king, or perhaps the one God loved the most. His son was Solomon, the wisest king.

I heard that story too Fannie. He was a great musician and a poet. He wrote the Psalms, some beautiful words. I sure can't live up to all of that.

No, she laughed, you cannot. But you are here with me now. I smiled at her.

So with her blessing, I decided to stay a while. We were in love. She taught me about horses – how to raise them, care for them, break them and train them. All I had been before that was a rider. Remember, I grew up as a coastal man who sailed on ships and was a foot soldier during the war. It was only when Joe and I stole John Drish's horses and rode to Ohio, I had any experience with the beasts.

Fannie loved to talk about horses. She told me Cortez brought them on a sailing ship to Mexico in 1493. Many died on the way. But they have survived on this land now for over four hundred years. The Mexicans bred them and raised them. Mustangs ran wild in herds on the American plains. The Comanche broke them and rode them. They are still here.

When me and Angus crossbred the Mustangs with our Kentucky thoroughbreds, the result was both speed and endurance. They are beautiful, tough sons-a-bitches. Those of us who live with them prefer them to humans most of the time she said.

Don't you think that's carryin' it a bit far? After all there was Angus and there is me.

She smiled at me coyly. Maybe. She pushed me onto the bed. That was the end of the conversation about horses.

She sold me a beautiful coal black filly, two years old, strong and spunky, just like the women I always fall for, at a fair bargain and me and Fannie parted friends. I held Fannie one last time and left her, a man with a satisfied mind. There is more to say about this I'll tell you later.

My horse's name is Maxine and she proved to be a trusty and faithful stalwart steed. I named her after Maxine Elliott who is a stage actress I admire. Her play *The Cowboy and the Lady* reminds me if I want to be a cowboy, I need a lady.

When Fannie and me struck our bargain about me buying Maxine, I started riding her around Denver. I bought her a fine leather saddle and looked for any opportunity to ride her to town to pick up some provisions or tools for the ranch. We started to become working partners real quick.

By the time I had settled in for a season with Fannie, I grew a full beard. It was whiter than my head of hair which still had a tinge of dark brown. Fannie didn't mind it. She said I looked like an old daguerreotype of General Lee. I told her that was wrong; I looked like General Grant only taller like Lincoln, but more handsome than him.

I read in the Denver paper about the Smuggler Mine in Aspen and how it was a big strike. The thought of that pulled on me and drew me to go out there.

One morning as the sun was coming up, I felt full of energy and restless. As I saddled up Maxine, Fannie was watchin' me while I averted her eyes. She saw me fasten my blanket roll behind the saddle this time. She knew this was the day I was leaving. We smiled at each other as I held her in a last embrace, neither of us speaking.

I grabbed onto the pommel and put my right foot in the stirrup. She saw me wince as I swung my left leg over the saddle. I sat looking at her eyes at last and shook the reins as we waved goodbye and I headed west.

From Denver City it was back in the saddle and due west to Aspen, a ways east of the territorial line with Utah at Grand Junction.

I thought about Fannie constantly. I had never stopped long enough to consider I could have stayed right there with her. I could have lived with her and helped her raise horses the rest of my life. But I didn't. My restless discontent drove me on further west. She knew that. She didn't try to hold onto me.

I had promised I would come back one day. It was about the talks we had together, about our blood going back over two thousand years ago when we were clans huddled together for survival just

45

north of Hadrian's Wall. Evidently the wall succeeded beyond the Romans' wildest dreams. For us, it was even better. It insured our isolation.

It was about our ceaseless journey, our unwavering courage. We face the world on our feet, never bowing down and kneeling before nobility. That was for the English spirit to admire, not us.

She helped me understand who I am and why I am. Our people had carried this country on our backs she had said. Our independent and self-reliant spirit is the American spirit she said. We are the hardest, toughest people on earth she assured me.

Fannie told me if anyone ever thought for one moment the Scots-Irish Confederates had fought to defend the plantation owners and their property, they were a fool. Without us, she said the Civil War would not have lasted a month.

She told me think of it this way David, the Scots-Irish had a fighting faith in America. I thought they certainly did.

Our all-but-invisible ethnic group has created the core beliefs of our American democracy; that our rights come from God, not the Government; all of us are born equal, and 'born aristocrats' don't exist, and if you tread on these truths, we will fight you down to the last broken bone, she said.

I looked at her face – full of resolve and purpose – and it was just like Joe's. But this was the face of a Celtic woman. Her long jet black hair was pulled back severely on top of her head and tied in a single braid in the back. Her piercing azure blue eyes were fierce and intent. There was no backing down or giving up in her. Hers wasn't a quiet, silent patriotism for certain either.

Centuries ago she would have been a warrior leader adorned with blue paint and tattoos, bare armed with a spear in her hand. Men would have feared her when she charged full force with her band of freedom fighters.

From what I know of my heritage and the history of my people in America, I knew for certain she was right. Still our spirit comes at a cost to others, like native peoples and Chinese immigrants. It is self-centered. But so what we say. Leave us alone to live our lives and we will leave you alone to live yours. None of it matters if I stay out of your way and you stay out of mine. Live and let live. It was then that I had had that conversation with Fannie about this.

———————◦———————

I told her, I said Fannie, it is one thing to stick up for yourself and not let someone take advantage of you. But it is another to hold a grudge and never forgive after the disagreement's issue is long over.

Fannie, right now in the papers, all over the country, they are writing the story of the blood lust feud between the Hatfield family in West Virginia and the McCoy family right across the Big Sandy River in Kentucky in what is called the Tug Fork region.

While there were earlier stories of strife and killings, the real troubles all started near the end of the Civil War when two friends, later the family patriarchs, were together in a Confederate unit fighting the Union in the Tennessee western campaign of the war.

When the Union was overrunning their outfit, William Anderson Hatfield stayed to hold them off while Randolph McCoy and the rest of his comrades got away. Later that night Anse showed up at their campfire much to their surprise. He announced he was done with the war and the fighting and he was leaving for home. Ole Ran said he couldn't break his vow and quit the cause like that. Anse left and went home anyway. Randolph stayed and, after his troop was decimated in another battle, spent the remainder of the war in a Union prison in Ohio. He came home a broken man more righteous and pious than ever before. He hated Anse Hatfield and his family.

47

After the war the troubles continued and escalated as they fought over a pig, land ownership, timbering rights, courtships and unsanctioned marriages of the young-ins across family lines. There were murders back and forth with no resolution.

It became a battle in the courts, with a lawyer on the McCoy side, a local judge on the Hatfield's' side and the Governor of Kentucky involved. Eventually it looked like a civil war was brewing between two states and legal claims were brought to the Supreme Court.

There was a New Year's Night Massacre this year and the Battle of Grapevine Creek back in 1880 which was just like a war between governments or states, where more than a dozen members of the two families was killed. The Governors of West Virginia and Kentucky threatened to have their militias invade each other's states.

Anse wanted peace while Randolph ultimately broke down, rebuked God and drank himself to a flaming fire of an end by himself in his cabin. There were tragic ends for many of their next generation and half of their progeny had been killed on both sides. I told Fannie all this.

She agreed with what I had said. She added that ancestry is always more complicated than it seems. Her MacAulay kinfolk claimed Gaelic-Norse ancestry as early Celts, along with the Lewis's, as their origin went way back in the old country, but she was not fair-haired like the Norse people. The spelling of the names of the families took on endless variations as time passed.

Her people, she said, got caught up in the Highlanders' feud between the Campbells and MacDonalds which was easily comparable to the Hatfields and McCoys here. The fighting and killing went back and forth for hundreds of years as the clans fought over power, land, religion, loyalty to the house of Bruce or Scotland's rightful king, autonomy of the highlands over the lowlands, and any other matters that occurred to them. The Campbells were always loyal to the idea of a king to rule over all of Scotland. The MacDonalds wanted a separate country of the Highlands.

The hatred, she told me, escalated until Robert Campbell ordered the massacre of the MacDonalds, including their women and children, at Glencoe in 1692. The Campbell clan was loathed throughout the Highlands after that. Over time the Campbells swallowed up the lands of my MacAulays as they had before with the MacGregors after first persecuting them for their differences. My MacAulays had accepted the leadership of the MacGregors and one strain of my kin had even sworn fealty to England's King Edward I. - the Scourge of Scotland.

That was how it was there she said. It is no different here. Brothers have been killing brothers since Cain and Abel. It is in Genesis.

I hear you Fannie, I said. I know we have been fighting each other forever. For me, I'm done with it. I am sick and tired of it. I have had half a lifetime of it – shedding blood for what good purpose?

She just looked at me dumbstruck with astonishment. Then her eyes turned warm and kind and she told me David, my dear man, I wish that you could. But my love, you cannot avoid it. We are human beings. There will come a day again when you will have to fight or want to fight sure as hell.

Deep down I knew she was right. Another time would come.

I asked Fannie how it was that her McAuley name sounded Irish, not Scottish. She beckoned me over to her rough wooden table in the kitchen and pulled out an old sheaf of papers from a cabinet. I could see they were very old letters and documents passed on over the generations.

The story of my people is old she said. It goes back and forth from Ireland to Scotland for centuries. Mine is just one variation of the long divergent line of kin. It is the one we brought with us to the new country. As you know, it was my name from my marriage to Angus. I was a Campbell. We were loyal to the king and hated by the Highlanders.

My husband's name might have been Macaulay at its root. There have been family members who spelled it Macauley, Macallay, Macalley, Macaullay, Macaully, Maccally, Maccaulay and Maccauly. It was MacAmhalghaidh, son of Amalghaidh, may have started it as an old Irish personal name. It gravitated to Dumbartonshire and became Hebridean in the northern isles.

There is more, much more, I could tell you about our history she said. Let me just say this:

The clan Alpin's tradition claims MacAlpin or MacAlpine is the oldest and most purely Celtic of the Highland clans, of royal descent from the dynasty of Kenneth MacAlpin who united Picts and Scots into one kingdom from the year 850 and transferred his capital to Perthshire from Dun Add in Dalraida - beside Loch Crinan. However, no clan of the name survived into the heyday of the clan system, though individual MacAlpins are recorded from the 13th century, mostly in Perthshire. Clan Mac Gregor claims origin from that royal MacAlpin stock: as also do MacAulay, MacDuff, MacFie, MacKinnon, MacNab and MacQuarrie.

"Mac" just means son of – MacDonald was son of Donald. Sometimes it is shortened to "Mc" like the Irish do. Sometimes it is just "M'".

In the Celtic tradition she said, the clan would "ingather" any stranger – of whatever family – who possessed suitable skills, maintained allegiance and, if required, adopted the clan surname.

Anyway, when Angus and me come to this country, we coulda give a shit less about all that old world life. I smiled at her and, after a moment, said you mean you could not of given a shit less. She just looked at me speechless for a quizzical moment. Then she got it and broke out laughing. Right you are wiseass lad she said.

But in a more serious moment she said David, it was our spirit we could never change. We carry it with us everywhere we go, over all of time, through all our generations. I understand you Fannie I said. That is what makes you wander, move on and keep seeking a better life. Sometimes it means you have to fight and conquer and win or die trying. I feel it too. For this I love you.

I'll tell you Fannie, my father Morgan did not have much interest in our roots from the old world. All I could get from him was that there were Wexleys in Ireland, Wales and England.

He knew we had been here for many generations and probably came over after the two first early settlements of English, but before the first revolution. That would make us Ulster Scots – Scots Irish. He supposed we might have been Ulster Scots but didn't know for sure. He was too busy making money as a banker.

Fannie I said, you know as well as I do how our country began. In the very beginning two groups of English settlers, our first British immigrants, came here and formed too tiny settlements. After they persevered, survived and began to thrive, the settlements became two huge territories – Massachusetts and Virginia. Eventually these splintered apart for religious, political, economic and philosophical reasons and became thirteen British colonies. As British citizens, we rebelled against our foreign king, fought the Revolutionary War and became this independent United States of America.

She smiled at me knowingly and nodded as she said, "I know all that too David."

But this is the important part I want to tell you, I said. We formed a government – our Constitution - as the best we could even with some ugly compromise. After General Washington finished his term as our first President, John Adams took over. His Vice President, who

51

was to become his lifetime rival, was Tom Jefferson. They were often civil to each other but spent some years not speaking to each other. It was because they had two different visions for our new American country.

Adams saw us as an urban mercantile society settling in small towns and cities which would become big cities in an urban country with manufacturing, trade and industry. For this he believed we needed a large powerful central government.

Jefferson saw us as a rural society, an agrarian one, with small yeoman farmers who owned their property and gradually settled the continent to the west. For this he believed we needed a very small and limited central government. The states would be more powerful and closer to the freedoms of the citizens.

In the end we became both of these things. At first the division was along regional lines – North and South. Eventually the rural and urban areas became mixed throughout the whole country. Many of us came out West, like you and Angus and me, for more freedom found on the rural frontier. We as Americans have always done that. But then most everywhere pockets of urban culture and society are formed and we become more crowded and less free. With too many people, I think America will always continue this way.

"I see what you mean and you have said it so simply and clearly. I agree that it is so.", Fannie said.

I also told her I heard the story about Hugh Glass who came from Pennsylvania and went to Montana and Dakota as an explorer and frontiersman in 1822. He went up the Missouri on a fur trading venture.

His parents were from Ulster and he was one tough son-of-a-bitch Scots-Irishman. He survived a grizzly bear attack and abandonment by his fellow company of hunters out near Fort Kiowa. It was reported in 1825 in *The Portfolio*, a Philadelphia literary journal and picked up by the newspapers. I read about it much later when I was a boy in Baltimore. It means so much more to me now than it did then.

Glass married a Pawnee and had a Scots-Irish-Pawnee American son. Both of them were killed and caused him a lifetime of sorrow. This is more evidence that we have always welcomed outsiders, or in this case they welcomed him, to join our clan and be part of our families. Glass spoke fluent Pawnee and witnessed the attacks against them by their enemies, the Lakotas and Cheyenne who eventually defeated them. They had fought the Comanche further south too. They nearly died out but by 1874 there were 4000 survivors pushed into the Indian Territory in Oklahoma.

Well you know who you are from the life you lead, she reminded me. I see through to your nature from the song of wanderlust you sing. You must see you are like me by now. I told her I do.

———————◦◦◦———————

While I came from Baltimore, traveled to places throughout the South, lived in Ohio and finally came out here, I realized that wherever I wander, by chance and happenstance, that is where I end up. Everywhere I have seen my people living, working, building, moving forward, enduring and building a whole country all across and throughout this great American land.

We are, and always will be, warrior poets, never stopping, never contented.

But the spirit of my kinfolk lives as close as it can to its ancestral Highlands - its hills, its lochs, its glens - somewhere in the Smoky Mountains and along the Tennessee River valley. Their ghosts endure there floating in the mists that rise above the crags and hollows and flowing with the streams of the waters.

The spirit lives there, protected once again from an intrusive civilization, behind its wall, as the remnant of Southern Appalachian culture, restlessly awaiting the next thing.

I felt and knew it deep down inside. It wasn't just because Fannie and I talked and she told me about it. I knew myself it was true. All this talk of clan and kin gives us a sense of something bigger, something greater we belong to, I had told Fannie in one of our last conversations.

I said, and as you say it teaches us who we are by our heritage and forbearers. I love you for this blessing you have given me by teaching me all this. Only at the first and last moment, for one step, we walk alone.

No matter where we wander, whoever we love, marry, or be with, who we know or befriend, we do not walk alone. We are born alone. We die alone. So wander, love, marry, be and befriend. But most important, know yourself the best that you can, the soonest you can. Be comfortable with yourself – in your own skin - because you do not walk alone.

Six – Freedom

Now I understand. It has taken me almost sixty years. Once I think about it in this way, it is so obvious. Before feudalism there was tribalism. Man lived in a natural state on the Earth. He had no concept of owning the land. It was God's Earth and man lived on it as he pleased. The state of man was more about the time in his story than the place.

This is how it was for the earliest people in Africa, in North America and pre-medieval ancient Scotland. The people lived in tribes or clans. There were few people and the planet was spacious.

The people gravitated toward a strong member in their clan-tribe-family for leadership. They fought willingly for him to protect their group from outsiders.

There was no organized society or need for it. The people were free as God created them, without even knowing the name for it – freedom. There were no nations, no cities and no governments. It was the natural state of man.

When man began to organize society, he made two significant conceptual changes – the ideas of land ownership and nobility. The Romans created a civilization of land ownership and dominance of nobility. The English did the same later.

Tribalism was replaced by feudalism. The peasants lived on the land claimed by the lords. They owed their fealty and their lives to him. This is what my Scots and Scots-Irish ancestors fought against in the late Middle Ages. Feudalism was slavery – the antithesis of freedom. My people came to understand that fiercely and have never stopped fighting against it.

The system of slavery, as it became in the South in my country, was a modern manifestation of English feudalism. The aristocratic planters were modern noblemen. Their slaves were their peasants. For them, this became the new natural order. For me and my people, it would never be.

Fannie was right. The white southern Confederates were not fighting to protect the noblemen, or their land, or their slave property rights. They were fighting as poor white farmers and mountain-dwelling clansmen against an invasion threatening to destroy their families and above all their freedom. A large powerful industrial government in the North was imposing nationalism on free people and their way of life.

I see that now. I understand that most of the Confederates I fought against, to preserve the Union and end slavery, were just like me. I had picked the right side to fight against slavery, but most of the enemy before me were not fighting for the preservation of feudalism and slavery. In terms of the numbers that fought, they were for the most part not the nobles.

While I had fought in the eastern campaign of the war – the Army of the Potomac under Generals McClellan and Burnside against the Army of Northern Virginia under Generals Lee and Jackson – mostly in Virginia and Maryland, I had little idea of what was happening in the western campaign along the Mississippi River. I had learned that after the fall of Vicksburg in '63, many Confederates had deserted and gone back to their homes. They found their families in deprivation and desperation, starving from the rampaging and pillaging their own Confederate government had done to them to re-supply their cause. They had been invaded by their own countrymen.

Jefferson Davis and R.E. Lee should have known half way through it with the loss at Gettysburg that their cause was hopeless. Their stubborn pride kept them going for two more years while they destroyed their own country as much as the invaders did. Desertion rates increased dramatically as the foot soldiers saw what was happening and understood the reality.

Some poor white farmers, like Newton Knight in Jones County, seceded from the Confederacy and waged war against them in defense of their own farms. Like so many non-slaveholding yeoman, he had been forced to join the Confederacy and was a cavalry Captain who fought at the Battle of Corinth. After that he deserted and changed sides. With a band of like-minded men, he waged guerrilla war on the Confederates with his small army of farmers and runaways in the swampy area near Hattiesburg and Taylorsville.

These men viewed the war from their Southern viewpoint as a rich man's war fought by poor men. Mississippi had passed a law that Confederates who owned twenty or more slaves were exempt from the fighting. So some poor whites like Knight enlisted runaway slaves to fight with them in the rebellion of the rebellion.

It was true there were many in the South as early as the 18th Century who hated the slaveholders and the institution of slavery as the Aristocratic class that it was. They had no intent to fight for their cause. They were poor and lived in isolation and knew they were looked down upon as a sub-class of white Americans. But the Appalachians and other remote areas were their Hadrian's Wall.

Most likely they viewed the invasion of the Yankees from the North as a more direct threat to their hard-scrabble, independent livelihood than they did the aristocracy in areas nearer by their own region. Therefore most of them fought for the Confederacy and its upper class white authority and the evangelical moral authority of its churches. Their choice was simple.

Slavery was coming to an end in the North. It was all but over there. Its system never fit in like it did in the agricultural South anyway.

That war should have been resolved between the two disparate peoples in the South, much as it was in ancient Scotland in the time of William Wallace; resolved by a groundswell of leadership from the peasants – black and white together – to overthrow the nobles. Maybe that is what John Brown thought he was doing.

As I said, I fought a war for the freedom of some while fighting against others for their freedom. War and freedom are more complicated and intertwined than they seem. One man's freedom is another man's bondage. War is cruelty and fighting it is useless. It rarely solves a problem.

Self-defense is another thing than aggression. War may be cruelty as General Sherman had said, but it may be unavoidable sometimes. It rarely solves anything right then and there at its outcome. Usually the end of a war is when the solution to a great problem can begin. At least that was true for my war.

There have been wars fought over a period of years over one or more issues about freedom. But there have been other wars fought on and off for centuries over the subjugation of a people, like in the old world.

Freedom and war go hand in hand all the way back to man's earliest existence, just as soon as he formed civilizations.

The South may have started the Civil War, or got tricked into it by their own decades of recalcitrance over slavery, fooling themselves about States' rights, but they fought a defensive war all the same.

For some like William Anderson (Anse) Hatfield, they got sick and tired of it and the Southern cause and walked away from it. For others like Newton Knight down in Jones County and other adjacent counties in the region of southwestern Mississippi, it was desertion too, but much more than that. Newt was a farmer, soldier and Southern Unionist who had fought in the war for the Confederacy at Corinth. He left the war when he learned that the horses on his farm had been taken by Confederates and his family had been hard pressed to keep up their farm.

He was joined by other disaffected men and freed slaves to form a band of guerillas in rebellion of the Confederacy. He was chosen as their captain. The small army lived and survived together fighting skirmishes against Confederates soldiers sent by General Polk to suppress their rebellious actions. Their hideout in the swamp was called "Devil's Den."

When his wife Serena separated from him, he fell in love and married a former slave named Rachel. Together they sired many children before they died.

He had determined that no country wanted them, so he supposed they had formed their own country. He declared its rules of self-government to be just four. Two of these were that a man kept what he put in and grew in the ground for himself and that a man is a man if he walked on two legs – simple as that.

After the war, as a Republican, the Union Army finally acknowledged him and tasked him with distributing food to struggling families in the Jones County area.

His epitaph said that he lived his life helping others.

———————————◦————————————

So I learned that freedom and war aren't simple and many strange things have happened in my country. Kinship and religious factors helped shape what we have done and became as Americans.

We should have left them alone and stayed out of their way. But we cannot change that now. What is done is done. All I want is to be left alone. Stay out of my way. I will do the same for you. Elsewise, I will pick a fight with you for my freedom.

Joe used to tell me, "Judge not, lest you be judged." I understand what he meant and where he learned it. So I can decide not to judge another person's actions, beliefs or treatment of me.

All the same, I can decide to demand that he leave me alone and get out of my way. That is not judging him. That is letting him live his own life and doing the same myself.

After the historic battle of Bannockburn, the Abbot of Arbroath declared to the pope in 1320:

For as long as one hundred of us shall remain alive we shall never in any wise consent to submit to the rule of the English. For it is not for glory we fight, for riches, for honors, but for freedom alone, which no good man loses but with his life.

Such was their resolve. Such was their refutation of central authority, their insistence on self-autonomy, independence, self-reliance and individual freedom. Free men they were.

Seven – Aspen

When I first came unto this country, I was already an old man. While I still get around fine on old Maxine's back, I had started to use a cane in my left hand to support my bad leg whenever I walked a distance. I'm still doing fine, but it helps to relieve the strain on my bad knee and atrophied calf muscle.

My experiences in Denver had been powerful and were illuminating. I will never see life the same again. It was what I learned about the West, its country and its people. It was meeting someone the likes of Darcy, and loving Fannie, and the love and appreciation of horses as the partners they are in life's journey.

Aspen is a man's town with a scarcity of women if you don't count the prostitutes camped out here to make their livin'.

It is astounding how life waxes and wanes in intensity. At times it comes at you so fast and all at once. Other times it comes along slow and sedate. I had fallen in love with two women in Denver, one for just an extraordinary day and the other for a passionate half of a year.

I try to remember those happy days of my life when I was a callow youth and life was so simple. It is sad that those times pass by and away, becoming a distant hazy memory of myself and life then.

But it passes away in the mists of time. Like a butterfly, it flutters before you a brief moment and is gone forever. War and hardship, cruelty and selfishness comes to us all after callow innocence is gone. With our clear-eyed harsher view as adults we still search for the goodness and try to remember.

John Donne said it so well. I have to give the English their due. He wrote in the 1600's that the bell tolls for us all. We are all connected. No man is an island.

It has been a while since I came out to Colorado in 1887. The East is far away and long ago. Out here everybody's a cowboy, even me a silver mine architect. I changed and adapted to the West and its people. It is wilder and freer – more breathing space.

If you want to understand Colorado, you got to go to the rodeo. This is how cowboys relax, show off, let off steam and compete. The circuit comes through here every year with traveling professionals and local hopefuls competing. They started the tradition in Mexico. The cattle drivers in Texas latched onto it.

There is calf roping, bull riding and steer wrestling. It's popular in Denver and they have been holding the Stampede over in Greeley for years now. The cattlemen there like to take a break between spring calving and summer haying to come to rodeo and test their riding and roping skills for prizes and braggin' rights.

I tried it figuring I've been riding horses for decades. It ain't so easy and certainly is a younger man's sport.

Colorado is a rugged mountainous place. I knew it would be before I came out here. But compared to where I came from back east, everything is bigger, sharper, clearer, fresher and more dramatic. What I did not expect was its connection to the New Mexico territory to its south and the Spanish speaking country below that border.

Out here it is about God, guns and country, maybe more about guns and less about God. What I like about it is the freedom. With no license or law, freedom is complete for the individual. But it is anarchy for the society. With too much law, there is no freedom. That is tyranny. I fought in a war for the freedom of some and against it for others, so I think about it some. Out here in the West, freedom leans mostly toward the anarchy side.

But the guns are necessary, particularly in a mostly lawless, wild place like this. Around here the Comanche will kill you if he is feeling mean-spirited and catches you alone. Further south in Texas and New Mexico, it is the Apaches to watch out for. If you can't take care of yourself, you are a goner. You have to be mindful of rattlesnakes everywhere in the open. Their bite will kill you if you don't pay attention. If you go out in the desert and are not well provisioned, you can die of starvation or thirst when there is no game or water. There are too many ways to die in the West.

I have my Army Colt from the war. Men like me in the infantry didn't have them. We had the old muzzle loaded muskets fixed with bayonets. But after the war, it was easy to buy the left-over revolvers the officers and cavalry had used.

I also bought a Hawken 50 caliber muzzle loaded, percussion cap, black powder, rifled carbine out here. They started making them back in 1820 before the Mexican War, but we were still using them near the end of my war, before the repeater carbines made by Henry and Winchester came out. They still make the muzzle loaders and my Hawken is about four years old.

I carry it in a saddle holster when I'm ridin'. We don't have any buffalo around here like out on the plains, but there are plenty of buck deer and goat, and sometimes wolves or mountain lion, to hunt in the hills up the mountains.

It is finicky though. Mine wasn't all it was cracked up to be. Half the time the percussion cap won't ignite the powder. I worry about that since I can't trust it will fire when I need it. It scared the hell out of me once when a Grizzly got too close to me. He ran off sure enough. Thank God.

On one trip south through the desert flats in New Mexico, I ran into an Apache war party. It was along the Rio Grande just north of Las Cruces. I spotted the six of them sitting horse on a mesa watching me ride through. I was close enough to see two of them had rifles set up on their legs and pointed toward the sky. I tried to look friendly while Maxine rode along, not making any moves toward my carbine in the saddle holster.

One of them, without a rifle, rode down toward me easy like without indicating his intentions. It was either his curiosity about a stranger or a feint with intent to attack. That is what the Apache do. They come at you one at a time if you are a lone rider. I guess it is their sense of honor or pride in their warrior abilities.

This was an attack. When he got a hundred yards from me, he changed from a trot to a full charge, whooping and wielding his tomahawk above his head. I didn't want to appear scared or put Maxine in harm's way, so I stopped and faced him.

When he got about twenty yards close, I pulled my Colt and fired at his chest. He dropped from his pony to the desert dust and I knew he was dead in his tracks.

I looked up at the others watching from the mesa and could see they were stirred up. They were all whooping and started moving down the mesa toward me. Forgetting their pride I guess, they all came after me together. The two with the carbines started firing.

Maxine figured out what was happening and took off at a sprint. I reined her toward an outcropping of rocks and she covered the quarter mile so fast the Apaches couldn't begin to catch up or get a bead with their rifles on the fast moving target.

We settled in the cover of the rocks and I dropped the first rider with my Hawken. The boom of the report from that 50 caliber big game rifle was so loud, and the sight of them losing their second brave, it took the spirit out of them. The remainder of the war party pulled up, turned around and charged off in the other direction. My war experience came in handy a few times out West.

Just east of here is the prairie. Settlers had been pouring in all the decades after the war, looking for land they could call their own to make a life as hard scrabble farmers and raise their families on their homestead. The problem there was the Indians. It was their land. But our government figured they could give it away to white pioneers to settle the rest of our country.

And we believed we could do whatever we wanted to the land as our Manifest Destiny. We cut timber, drilled mines and built railroads all over the West to make the travel across the whole country a practical reality.

The mighty Sioux Nation inhabited this land once- the Santee, the Yankon and the Yankonai, and the Lakota. Of these, the Lakota dwelled on the prairie as the great horsemen, buffalo hunters and mighty warriors.

We fought them in the Dakota War of 1862 north of here where 303 Santee Sioux were tried for their offenses against white settlers. President Lincoln commuted death sentences for 284, while 38 were hanged in Minnesota. Treaties and annuities were suspended. Some moved to the Crow Creek Reservation in Missouri.

Red Cloud fought the United States in the Wyoming and Montana Territories from 1866 to 1868. Again in 1876-1877 the Great Sioux fought the U. S. Military with the Cheyenne as their allies.

In 1890, just after I came out here, the Lakota were massacred at Wounded Knee. At the end of the century, I have seen the hired hunters, working for the railroads, slaughter the Buffalo to near extermination. They did it for sport and as a strategy to starve out the Indians and make them give in to our will.

The Santee and Lakota, proud Sioux people, starving and defenseless, were driven off the prairie and forced to move to reservations.

It was our Manifest Destiny that motivated us to believe we were entitled to this whole hemisphere. We knew the completion of the western railroads would make it all possible once we got the Indian problem resolved.

It began when Jefferson pushed them out of the East across the Mississippi. Then Jackson pushed them out of the South. Harrison herded them into Oklahoma which the white man had defined as Indian Territory. The Dawes Act and Homestead Acts gave 160 acres to settlers and removed land from tribal ownership under Federal authority. Lincoln and his successors finally destroyed them in the West.

Back in 1880, the reservations were established under the Treaty of Fort Laramie in 1868. It was so heartbreaking and sad, I have no words. We destroyed the once proud indigenous people of this land. And it was all unnecessary. There was plenty of room for everyone.

The many years that drifted by in Aspen, I ran my business and traveled south whenever I could.

But when I was in Aspen, I began to withdraw from people and just watched over my crew when I had to. So in 1891 I bought some land up the slope and built a cabin. Aspen appeared below me like a bowl or a saucer.

Maxine liked it up there. She had her own corral to run around in. We still needed to ride together, more her than me. I built her a quarter mile track around the corral and gave her a race when she wanted it.

I made a small stable and barn for her, secure from wolves or coyotes at night. There was a water trough and some extra space for her feed and grooming. Once I had civilized and outfitted my little plot for her and me, I made some creature comforts in my cabin for my solitary self.

I ain't touched a drop of whiskey in ten years, just a beer once in a while with my boys in town. For too many years Lady Whiskey kept me company and I loved her so well. She damned near destroyed me. My excuses for it had been lost women and the cruel war. Finally, I chose to live and it worked out better to part company with her.

Over time I collected a library of books shipped in from Denver or the east. These were my friends I needed the most. I contemplated mortality and the verities of humanity and was pleased. The life of solitude and the outdoor beauty around me was enough – more than enough.

It was time to settle up and sum up what it had all meant. It had meant Morgan and Josiah and Fannie most of all. These spirits were of the past.

William Blake was a peaceful comfort by the fire on cold winter nights. The Songs of Innocence and the Divine Image brought gentle thoughts. The Songs of Experience rang truer to life – Tiger, tiger burning bright – life and death if I die.

I read the poets Tennyson, Donne, Milton, Whitman, Yeats and Twain. Browning and Dickinson were too sloppy sentimental for me. I read Herman Melville's Moby-Dick and remembered the smell of the sea and that my old friend Josiah had read it when he was a slave.

Melville had spent years at sea like me and had said, "Faith, like a jackal, feeds among the tombs, and even from these dead doubts she gathers her most vital hope."

Joe had my journals so I had to remember my life as a sailor best I could without them. It was better he had them to remember me by. I could still smell the salty brine.

Reading and contemplating in the quiet tranquil solitude of the evenings at home in the 1890's, I saw that life is incongruity, inconsistency, and contrast if I stop to think about the unknowable connection between the people on Earth now at my time and times before –like the sootbleakened night under the gas lamps of Victorian London where the sandstone on the buildings has become chemically bonded with the smoke from coal burned in homes and spewed from chimney stacks of the infancy of man's early industrial age, or the clarity of the air and the light at sunrise and the way the face of the Rockies look from Aspen just after the spring runoff of snowmelt from its peaks in the same 1890's, or the savanna grasses vast across the plains of Africa when man first contemplated life on this Earth millennia before; contemplated his immortal soul and place as a speck in the cosmos for the first time.

I had seen most of my country and learned from my Love those important parts of the old country I had never seen- but seen enough through her eyes for me. I know who I am.

As I have spent time alone in my cabin, the quiet evenings have given me time to think. In reflection, in trying to understand the meaning of my life, I have turned back to the study of history once again as I did in my youth with Morgan.

From reading I have learned to put in perspective what I have experienced in my own life. Historiography has taught me what different historians have thought about an historical event or person over time. Different historians have viewed these things differently over time – perspective.

With the reading of exegesis books I have learned what different writers have thought about the writing of the great writers – perspective.

I have learned to embrace perspective to gain understanding. At first we are repulsed by perspective since the shallow view of it is that it is opinion and we always dislike the opposing opinion of others. We call it bias, prejudice or other derogatory names when it is really just a range of viewpoints.

I believe the more we look at the perspective of others and consider the variety of viewpoints, the more we learn. In the end, when we consider the actions of humans, we see that the truth is the sum of all of it. The understanding of it, with all its acrimony, has brought me more peace as ironic as that seems.

For example: *War is cruelty. There is no use trying to reform it. The crueler it is, the sooner it will be over.* When General Sherman said that he understood the nature of war, its inevitability and how to fight it better than the rest of us. The newspapers called him a lunatic – perspective.

Some have said that learning is a process like peeling back the layers of an onion – the deeper you go, the more you learn the truth. Others have said that all it is is an onion – all the way to its core. Maybe it is the layers that are the truth and the goal is not to get to the core. The truth is simpler than we imagine.

Fannie's truth was a settled truth in her mind. She had no doubts. There were no conflicts in her view of who she was or what her life meant to her. God bless her for her assuredness in her beliefs.

Eight – Sonora

After some time, whenever I needed a change of scenery, which for me was often necessary, I would saddle up and slide down into the New Mexico territory. It was still a territory then. It might become a state after a few more years.

The ride is an easy time, just 250 miles south down along the Continental Divide and parts of the Santa Fe Trail to Santa Fe, about a six-day ride. The El Camino Real de Tierra Adentro is near Santa Fe and connects to San Juan, New Mexico all the way south to Mexico City along the Rio Grande River.

When a lone western man travels around like I do, he gets to see the vast natural beauty of the deserts and the distant vistas of the mountains. It is a different beauty than the East and different from the South as well. You get to love the rich bright oranges, yellows and browns as a change from the greens of the grasses and forests back east of the Mississippi.

And the land is so open and un-impeded. You can see for miles across it to the horizon. The sky is bigger to the eye in the daytime that I could ever have imagined. In the black chill of night there are more stars in the heavens than anything I have ever seen. Guess that's why many become desert rats. This great land of ours is so big you can never see it all in its extent or diversity.

When you are standing outside on a clear night in Denver at a high elevation, or more so in Santa Fe which is a high desert with the mountains less a part of the panorama, the sky takes on a special difference. It is like you are alone on a flat platform with the sky full of countless stars. It is all and everything you can see. There is a sense you can feel, a vastness beyond belief.

The terrain has no obstruction of tall trees or buildings like in the East or even the South. There is no interference from other sources of light. It is you and the universe in the cosmos.

I remember it was like that on the ocean standing watch on my clipper ship as a boy. When the sea is calm, it was the same flat platform and the same Northern Hemisphere sky where rarely the colors of the Northern Lights – Aurora Borealis – appeared. It is then you know how small we are as an immeasurable speck of the whole thing. You cannot help but be humble.

The daytime is a different world and the differences in the West, the East and the South are apparent. Man must have known this same thing since the beginning of time in this world.

Maybe that is part of the attraction of the West for me, as it was for the ocean when I was a boy. Life is a circle as well as a cycle.

Santa Fe is in the mountains. You have to climb up a gradual elevation until you are on a high desert plateau. It is eight thousand feet above sea level – three thousand feet higher than Denver, the mile-high city.

It is the same with the diversity of the people as the diversity of the land; and I include in that the Indians and the Mexicans. It is their land and country just as much as or more than it is ours. Somehow I was taken in by their Spanish language and their descendants here in what is now our territory of New Mexico. The Mexicans are a lot like me – independent, self-reliant, capable people able to survive hardship. They have endured on this land longer than we have and I learn a lot about that from them.

That is truly why I consider so many of them in Santa Fe my friends. They have endured both the Spaniards and the Americans and they have the survival skills. They are still here. I enjoy the relaxations with my Mexican friends and I have come to have many. We sit back in the cantinas for their Tequila, my beer and some talk.

We love to swap stories and tall tales, even if they are exaggerated and some not true.

They all know me in Santa Fe when I pass through. My friends there have names like Juan and Pedro. They have a sleepy, peaceful Spanish heritage there coming from Mexico, dating way back to the first colonists in 1610. The only other town coming from the Spanish that is older is St. Augustine in Florida. They came there to settle in 1565. Anyway, Santa Fe is the oldest American settlement I guess.

The people in Santa Fe, like the people in Mexico City and all of Mexico for that matter, are a mix of the high born Castilian Spanish and the indigenous native Indians. They have crossbred for hundreds of years but still have a caste system of two tiers.

In Santa Fe the old deep roots are evident. The Spanish high born descendants hold the provincial government positions and rule the territory locally despite the involvement of the United States since the Mexican American war and despite its independence from Spain before that.

So the people are a mix of low born Mexican Indians and high born Spanish nobles. It's another example of feudalism I see the world over. But I like the people and they are generally very friendly to Gringos like me when I visit. It was there in Santa Fe, because of the time I spent there with the locals, I learned the Spanish language. The people have more respect for an outsider when you speak to them in their language. Hell, the Indians had to learn it generations ago to get along in their own country.

They hold celebrations and fiestas all the time to celebrate their proud heritage. It will always be a part of the Southwest reaching way up into Colorado and across Texas.

The Mexicans were the first cowboys on the continent. There is much for me to discuss about horsemanship with my friends there. I'm knowledgeable now about breaking and training horses and share that with the Mexican people who have done that since the Spaniards introduced them to horses centuries ago. I have that in common with these horse people and the Indians as well. Their Gauchos were cowboys herding cattle before my people ever were.

If I had it to do all over again, I would have been in the cavalry, not the infantry, during the war. I couldn't then though because I was a city boy from Baltimore.

From there it is an easy drift into Mexico, another 250 miles down to the border at El Paso. I stay there for a day or two to look up some old friends.

I met James Longstreet once in El Paso. Old Pete had settled in New Orleans after the war but was out west trying to get investors for a new railroad from New Orleans to Mexico.

He was Bobby Lee's most brilliant tactician and strategist and I told him so. He was very gracious about it and thanked me for my service to the country. I had marveled at how smart he had been like a master chess player who could see six moves ahead. Old Pete could look at the events leading up to and the layout before a battle and almost see into the future. He was most always right. This made him too guarded and pessimistic for Lee's liking. But Lee respected him. He had to. His brains offset Lee's brashness and surely saved his chief commander's bacon on more than one occasion.

Unfortunately he had taken most of the blame for the Confederate loss at Gettysburg. He just knew Pickett's charge was foolhardy and he said so in no uncertain terms. He had been right.

Longstreet had been a lifelong friend of Grant's going back to their early days as cadets at West Point. They always had respect for each other's brains, grit and ability. The South grew to dislike Old Pete for selling out his southernness when he became a Radical

Republican arguing for Reconstruction and equal rights after the war.

It was strange to meet General Longstreet in El Paso of all places. But it made sense. The big Georgian, Old Pete, had been dealing with the new post-war reality. El Paso was the major border town in Texas. Americans and Mexicans were crossing back and forth between the two countries all the time. Just across the Rio Grande was Ciudad Juarez in Chihuahua, Mexico.

The United States and Mexico wanted to do business. There was a growing cooperation for each country to gain a benefit. That is what we had begun doing in America the last hundred years. After conquering a region, maybe with a war to decide the more powerful, then we wanted to do business. We call that progress.

The Anglo and Mexican-Spanish cultures and languages were blending. Longstreet knew that. He was a smart man and always had been a forward-looking progressive thinker. Now he was fixing to build a railroad between the two countries. I'll bet Old Pete did it too.

Anyway, it had been an honor to meet the old General and I wished him well. I never minded talking about the war with anyone who had been in it since they understood what it was really like which no outsider ever could. When we talked about it he acknowledged that, for the common Confederate foot soldier, it was a rich men's war fought by poor men. I couldn't help but admire him for understanding that.

As for Texas, you know it became a Republic in 1836, having fought its own war with Mexico's Santa Anna. It was its own country, independent of Mexico and the United States, until it was annexed to the United States ten years later in 1846. Then it fought in the U.S.-Mexican War until 1848. Just twelve years later it joined the Confederacy in 1860 and fought for its independence once again.

So Texans are fighters and fiercely independent people. But they learned to cooperate and accept Spanish speaking Mexican people as part of their cultural heritage. Their language, food and traditions blended together.

Sounds like my people doesn't it? That's why I have always gotten along so well with them. In west Texas it is generally peaceful and friendly.

But I like to cross the border and travel deep into Mexico to immerse myself there with their people. My favorite town is Hermosillo – it means little brother - down Sonora way. It is just another 400 miles southwest from El Paso across some rugged country. That's the hardest part. I don't mind it. Hardship has been the story of the life I have chosen.

These are great distances to cover on horseback. I am gone from Aspen for weeks at a time. Fortunately my job and my crew allow me to do that. I can wander to my heart's content. It is the going I need. It has been so for some time. Fannie knew it.

The Continental Divide passes through Chihuahua in Mexico. I break off before that and swing west to Hermosillo. Hermosillo is a backwater of a desolate desert – if there is such a thing – with heat, dust, cactus, sunshine and quiet desperate poverty, horses and burros. It isn't much of a watering hole.

There aren't any ex-patriot Americans there. Probably there are some in Mexico City. Fact is the Mexicans are still sore at us from the Mexican-American War. They aren't very welcoming to gringos because they lost nearly half of their country from that war. We took a lot of new territory into the United States that would later add states to the Union – and the Confederacy.

I did get all the way down to Mexico City once. It is a huge city set in a bowl of a valley surrounded by mountains and always full of political unrest. I saw the ancient pyramid or temple there from when the city was called Tenochtitlan in 1325, right in the middle of town as a memorial to the mighty Aztec civilization before Cortes killed Montezuma and destroyed it in 1520.

I didn't know anybody there but met a group of Americans. They were living together in an enclave and I ran into them in the cantinas. They were mostly veterans from the Civil War down there to work together on that end of Longstreet's railroad. There they were, graybacks and bluecoats together getting along and putting the past behind them. It was gratifying to join them and see my Americans together as my countrymen.

The concentrated mass of humanity in Mexico City is impressive. Chicago pales by comparison. As you know, I'm not much taken by big cities and neither is Maxine. She gets jittery around so many people and so do I. We left after a few days and headed west into the desert toward the Baja.

For me the trip to Hermosillo is worth it though. They know me there and it feels like home. In Rosa's Cantina, I gather up my friends for some braggin' talk and a glass of beer. Rosa is smart as a whip – or at least cunning – and mean as a rattlesnake.

She has to be to handle that crowd in her cantina. Rosa is plump, average height, wears her black hair short and never changes the stern passive expression on her face no matter what anybody says or does. She looks like she hates all her fellow human beings. It takes some time to see through that mask and come to know she runs her place because she cares about people.

Rosa was about the same age as me, a little older than my Fannie McAuley. I visited her cantina every few months and conversed with her in her Spanish tongue. I came to know her and recognize she was a good person at heart, just tryin' to make a livin' and get by. I never saw a husband and figured he had been gone for some time. Rosa came to like me and see that I was a good man who could be trusted even though I am an Anglo.

So when I took a fancy to her daughter Maria, Rosa was fine with that. She knew her daughter Maria was strong, no wilting flower, and could take care of herself. Now for some reason Maria found an attraction in me. I don't know why. Maybe it was the curious love of a stranger, a mysterious cowboy from up north who was different and stood out from the men in town. Maybe she looked up to me like a father figure. Like me, without a mother, I could understand that. A fondness and affection grew between me and Maria while her mother Rosa watched.

Her daughter Maria is the finest example of sweet, Spanish womanhood my eyes have ever had the pleasure of gazing upon. Rosa's girl Maria is mi' amour *mi' corazon* - my heart and paramour. Spanish is a loving tongue.

It is peaceful, usually, but I got in a gunfight there once. The way it happened was this. But first, before that, Maria and I had been upstairs in her bedroom and living quarters above the cantina.

After a quiet dinner together - some tamales, chili con carne and rough red wine - we had looked into each other's eyes and knew we had a deep need, more than an itch, to go upstairs. I followed up the stairs behind her watching her loose dress sway from side to side from its gorgeous round pivot point at her waist. As I climbed the stairs, I looked down to the floor and saw Rosa busy at the far end of the bar pouring a customer a shot of Tequila. Our eyes came in contact, and Rosa gave me a faint smile – a quick knowing look with a subtle hint of acceptance - before she turned back toward the customer.

Upstairs in Maria's room, door closed tight, she threw her arms around me and pressed her soft flat belly and strong thighs against me hard. She moaned and looked at me with a painful expression. Clearly her need was as great as mine.

Now Maria is no child. I am not her first rodeo ride and won't be her last. We have an understanding when I come down Sonora way.

She is much younger than me and may look twenty but she is a perfectly preserved much older woman than that.

Our time together is more than sensuous; she is funny. She points at this old cowboy's body while she caresses me gently with her infectious smile.

I look at her smooth brown voluptuous body with curly black hair in all the places where it is supposed to grow. It glistens at the sweet place between her charming thighs.

It doesn't take us long to get down to business when we are both feeling like that. I picked her up and bounced her on the bed, her hair flying away from her beautiful head. Her face is so gorgeous, I'm on the bed on top of her before the bed stops bouncing.

She had just enough time to throw her dress over her head and no need to remove underwear which she does not wear. I managed to kick off my boots, pull off my shirt and britches, including my underwear, but not enough time to worry about my socks.

We ride fast and together and before you know it we are lying side by side, her head tucked against my shoulder. Thank you David. Thank you Maria. Sweet Jesus she treats me so right.

She had a sit-up copper bath tub she kept in her room. When we got done she called for a family employee to bring up buckets of hot water. We took turns having a bath, washing each other and freshening up before dressing and going back downstairs. After we got situated at a table, that's when it happened.

Maria was sitting on my lap at a table sharing our beer and in comes a mean lookin' hombre. He was a big man carrying a lot of weight. I could see he was lookin' for trouble. Maria gave me that look with those laughing eyes that said 'David, stay out of it'.

The hombre' talked his way into the poker game at the big table. I knew trouble was comin'. Before long everybody started hollerin' at the hombre' for cheatin'. It was gonna' be a gamblin' fight.

He got red in the face and bolted up on his feet. He cursed at them and threw the table over. All the silver and cards flew around and bounced on the floor.

I set Maria down and got up to help. I said whoa there compadre, settle it down. He wheeled toward me and didn't say nothin'. He must have thought I was an easy mark, being a skinny gringo with a crippled leg. But I'm wiry and wily and I carry an equalizer too. I am an old man now, but still have a young man's spirit.

He started to draw and I grabbed my Army Colt fast as I could. His shot was first. He must have been nervous because it missed by a mile. Mine put a '45 right in the center of his chest. He dropped over onto his back on the floor. The blood began pooling around him on the rough planking.

Maria said I'd better beat it out of there fast before the sheriff comes. We stood up close together there in the middle of the room. All eyes were on us and it was quiet as a tomb. No one moved. It was like a daguerreotype still picture.

Rosa was slowly wiping the bar counter with a wet rag. She looked at me and nodded her head just slightly, almost imperceptibly. I touched the brim of my Stetson and nodded toward her in return.

Maria's sad eyes looked up at mine one last time. I looked at her beautiful face, and whispered, *dime porque lloras* (tell me why you're crying). She breathed into mine, *de felicidad* (of happiness).

She knew I had to go. She insisted on it for my safety. She loved me enough to let me go. My greatest loves had always done that when the time came. But her feelin's were of happiness for the thought of me. So were mine for the thought of her. So many of my loves were as much about an idea – romanticism - as they were about the reality.

That was the last I ever saw her, mi' amour *mi' corazon*. I often miss her, but I can't cross the line anymore. I strode out of the saloon, jumped on Maxine and she galloped out of Hermosillo heading northeast toward the border.

It is not nearly possible to describe how a man feels when he truly loves a woman - what he would go through, how far he would ride, what he would do to be with her – or more than one in a man's lifetime. My Maria is irreplaceable, one of a kind like Fannie. I would ride through hell itself, across the lonely desert with distant howling coyotes, from countless sunrises to sunsets, to find her and be with her.

In sleepy Mexico the deep religious Christianity in the people and their old missions in the dusty desert towns going back to the time of the Spanish is all part of these loving and passionate folks.

I'm not foolin' myself. She has had and will have other men. We can't be together all the time or forever. That changes nothin'. She loves me without any doubt. Our feelin's are strong and burnin' inside us. Her face is painted in front of my eyes when I ride with Maxine across the deserts and mountains to get there and hold her.

It is powerful and I wouldn't avoid these feelin's even if I could. She is a miracle, a dream and she is real – my Maria. I am a lonely dreamer but I love you.

As far as the women go, I guess I'm still thinking like a sailor. I have a girl in every port. I get to spend time with my special woman when I am in each town. I am a romantic wanderin' loner who falls in and out of love at the drop of a hat; or so I lead myself to believe. But I never forget a one of them. It is building up good memories to displace all the bad stuff from the war years that have taken me so much time to get out of my head.

81

The brown-eyed beauties like Maria in Hermosillo fairly take my breath away. And I must admit, my penchant for my big infatuations with the Senoritas is that loving Spanish language for the most part. Every girl I spend time with is my love for the time I am there.

But really this is just a fantasy feelin'. There have been only three women I have really truly loved in my life. There was Estelle Culpepper, my colored beauty back in Ohio, Fannie McAuley, my kindred spirit in Denver, and Maria my Senorita in Sonora.

Certainly though I am drawn to women with an intensity. It must be because I was raised without a mother. I must be always looking for her.

Fannie felt the closest I ever got. Estelle and Maria were younger and drove my man's passion for beauty. Darcy was just a beautiful idea – a picture in my mind like a beautiful sky, or mountain slope or a sunset.

As far as what I had done there in Hermosillo, as I remember Fannie, she had found the balance between the hateful mind and the loving heart. The hateful mind rails at the hypocrisy, and the irony of that, in human creatures. The loving heart forgives and forgets as it leads us forward through life. We must forgive, starting with ourselves. It must be so for us to die in peace.

And I believe she had taught me to do the same at the end. The mind sees the ugly in the humans of this world, but the heart sees the beauty in us all.

Anse Hatfield, Josiah Ashford and William Wordsworth all came to that understanding if only finally at the end. I can imagine that the commanders in the war and most of the rest of us did too ultimately.

Nine – The Mine

I came out here for a fresh start and a new lease on life. The rush was on for gold in California and silver in Colorado. Friends had told me Aspen was the place to go and strike it rich. It was a lawless, rowdy and dangerous place, but no more difficult for me than I had seen in the Merchant Marines or the war.

I figured my carpentry and architectural design skills would fit in somehow. Turns out the mining companies were in desperate need of help in designing, fabricating and installing wooden beam support structures in the deep tunnels.

The mining company wanted to hire me as an employee. But you know me and know I never could work for an employer for wages. So I hired a crew of seven men and started my own company. We had to cut timber and use it to fashion our beam and post structures. The timber is mostly soft wood out here and we had to factor that in to the load bearing capacity.

My crew had come out here from all parts of the country, some from the East and South and two nearby in Missouri. Jeff Grady and Frank Dell were my best hands. I could put Jeff in charge when I was away and didn't have to worry. He had the leadership skill and Frank had the best work skill. Both of them were younger than me and had the strength and energy we needed.

Jeff was average height and stocky-built with hard hands. He had tousled light sandy hair and a fair complexion. His pale blue eyes had a softness when he spoke to you. There was a kindness in his face and I knew he understood people almost intuitively.

Frank was taller and wiry with that black Irish look about his dark eyes. He reminded me of me when I was much younger and my hair was fuller and dark brown. He was serious and dependable. These were strong men who had seen some life and I was fortunate to have them.

I put Jeff in charge of the day-to-day activities and deployments, but in an effort to be democratic I met with both of them together every couple days at the saloon to have some fun and talk about our projects. We drank together but none of us had a drinkin' problem. That would have gotten in the way and I couldn't stand for it.

My crew were a good bunch. Sam McNabb had come out here on his own to speculate. When that didn't work out, he came to work for me. After about a year he left to go back to Missouri because his wife had turned ill and needed him back home.

Joe Johnson was a black man who had settled here with his wife and four kids. He was smart as a whip and strong as an ox. I left him in charge of the timbering operation.

Earl Thomas was not the brightest but he gave me an honest day's work, week in and week out. He was dependable.

When trouble came, I could count on Henry Wallace to be right by my side. As much as you know me, I would back down from a fight before he ever would. Sometimes that came in handy. I was too old to be the bodyguard for these young men in every situation.

I understand and expect that these young men are going to do some gamblin' and whorin'. That's fine, but the work we do is dangerous and we have to pay attention.

These men, like most of the rest, had come poor looking for gold. But the gold rush days were over and silver mining was different. You can't pan for it and if you don't have the money to finance a mine, you end up working for somebody. My boys understood that and understood my feelings about that authority thing too. We got along fine. Yep, they worked for me for wages, but it would never be a corporate thing.

Another of my crew was John Knowland. His family homestead was in New England. I learned later that his father had fought with the Massachusetts regiment under Burnside's Expeditionary Corps. His father had died in Andersonville while I was there. John had been just a boy when he lost his father. He wanted me to tell him everything I could remember about it. I told him I don't want to talk about it, but I'm sure his father fought bravely because we all did.

You see, I had no way or anything I could say to this man who had lost his father. First, I didn't know his father personally. Second, how would any description I could offer about my experience at Andersonville console him? Last, we who were in it could discuss it together in terms that made us feel better about it. That is because we were there and understood it. It was easier to share experiences with Confederates, common foot soldiers like me on the other side, than with anyone who was not there. No, I just had to tell this young man his father was brave and had an honorable death. That was a lie of course.

When I look at my men and think about how we work and relate together, it makes me remember something else Fannie and I talked about. It was important, more and different than our negative view of authority. It was the idea of the egalitarian view. Of course we are not all equal. No two men are the same in all regards. We all have different talents and gifts, souls and demons, strengths and weaknesses.

But we are naturally equal in our human rights. We are not given equality by some authority, just equal opportunity and treatment. Some men will rise to the top and some won't. Fannie often

85

reminded me that our country was formed on that basis and that our ancient ancestors believed it too.

We agree with the egalitarian view looking up from the bottom. No man is our superior and we are no man's inferior.

Our Scots-Irish President Andrew Jackson believed in that. As a frontiersman, he had a pride in his capability and self-sufficiency city people back East would not understand. With their refined manner, they dismissed his value and looked down on him as crude and inferior. His was a new idea of democracy based on that populist egalitarianism.

Because of that – our egalitarianism – we have always included new members into our extended clan. The Scots-Irish have married outsiders. Our progeny has produced Americans with African and Indian blood mixed with our own. Like I said before, we were all tribal people. We all hold the same spirit. Now it is the American spirit.

———————◦———————

For our work I needed to learn something about rock – geology – to figure out the loads, stresses and strengths required. There is mostly solid granite in these here mountains. It is only weakened by the silver veins and pockets running every which way at locations we couldn't identify. In Colorado we were called "hard rockers" because of this. The silver was the source of fault lines to consider, which we couldn't, for the pattern the explosions would produce.

South of here in Nevada, Arizona and other places like the San Juan's the rock composition is a softer mix and made up of volcanic igneous rock with maybe sandstone and limestone.

86

So with the variation of hardness, strength and weight, for us it was trickier and more dangerous.

While I had studied architecture and engineering back in Ohio, the physics of the geology involved with mining and mine safety was somewhere far afield. I read what was available and learned what I could, but most of it was experimental and based on experience and judgment. I did all I could.

They use Chinese immigrant workers to set the nitro when they blast deeper into the tunnels because no white man wants to handle that volatile stuff. I had to be responsible for certain aspects of mine safety. It was all tied together.

When they work deeper into the mine, they make planned explosions to break rock and open up the mine deeper in. The explosions yield broken rock they carry out with manual labor – the Chinese again – to bust it up further and examine for silver veins and content.

If busting up the rock doesn't reveal or release the silver, the rest of the process requires smelting. Furnaces heat the busted rock and also use a chemical reducing agent to decompose the ore. This drives off other elements as gases leaving the slag and separated metal behind. Coke or charcoal are commonly used as the reducing agent and produce carbon dioxide and carbon monoxide which kills more mine workers at the smelter.

That all works fine most of the time, but the stresses from the explosions travel beyond the site of the explosion and often cause unexpected cave–ins. This is where my structure supports come in. They are supposed to maintain the integrity of the tunnel.

It isn't foolproof. We don't have the information for the complex pattern of strengths and weaknesses throughout the veins in the rock. We are constantly rebuilding our structures and sometimes burying the dead – usually the Chinese.

The other problem we faced was a people problem. The owners would watch the workers for "high grading" which is where they steal and sneak out bits of silver in their lunchbox or concealed in their clothing. It is illegal theft and men have been hung for it.

I worked for the Smuggler Mine up on Smuggler Mountain. It had been the biggest and they took out a silver nugget weighing 2,054 pounds. We did find the veins of silver and the mine yielded rich deposits. In time the owner and his investors became filthy rich.

The kind of engineering I learned was hands-on, built from experience. It always got me in trouble with the corporate types. These were the men who sat behind desks far from the mining operations. That had fine academic educations and understood theory but never its practical applications. When I would argue with them and fight over what must be done, I never got anywhere. I couldn't change them. It was up to them they said. I didn't get to decide they told me. My only solution to this conundrum of communication was to move on when I got fed up.

When the Smuggler Mine had worked out and came to an end, I contracted out to other mines – the Sheep Mountain and Bear Mountain mines - and drifted along as the years passed.

It is so beautiful here in the Rocky Mountains. I like the springtime the best. After the snow melt off, it warms up and the colors are vibrant up in the hills and peaks contrasted with the azure blue sky and white billowing clouds.

But it became once again like my youthful years in Baltimore before the war. I kept occupied building things, and had friends, but it didn't feel like home. I was still discontented.

All those years in Aspen I thought about Denver but I never went back. The years rolled along and too soon it was too late. We walk alone. It was regrettable, and even inexplicable, but we come into this world alone and that is how we leave it. In the end we walk alone.

Ten – Revelation

After too many years, in the spring of 1899, I went back to Denver to see Fannie. For so long I had wanted to go back, but now it would be difficult to know what to say. How would I explain my long absence and my reappearance? She had willingly let me go. She had no intention of standing in my way to stop me. That's why I loved her. But how would she feel now? What would it be like between us?

We rode east toward the rising sun early in the morning after daybreak. Maxine sensed something as we headed toward Denver. There was something strange in the old girl's behavior. She whinnied and turned her neck as though to lead me in another direction. She was excited like the filly she was ten years ago.

About ten miles out the terrain looked familiar as an old habit. Maxine recognized the surroundings and began to gallop. Within sight of the ranch I said we are almost home girl.

When we arrived at the long straight entry road, with the white split rail fence along the side, she broke into a sprint. For the last mile, lathered up, heart pounding, she flew like the wind. I leaned into her bending forward as far as I could and buried my face in her powerful neck. Go old girl I told her. Give it everything.

As I raced with her closer and closer to our objective, my mind's eye saw her, anticipating the joy to hold her again. It was but a moment ago I looked back and left her, an eternity awaiting to see her once more.

We landed at her home in a whirlwind cloud of dust. At the ranch house gate, it didn't say McAuley. The name had changed. The people there told me she had passed away three years ago from a winter ague that turned to pneumonia. My heart fell in that moment and my mind was consumed in disbelief by its old companion melancholy once again.

They didn't know who I was but mentioned she had had a son. He lived in closer by town where a family close to Fannie had taken him in.

Darcy Farrow Wilcox had raised him with her husband Henry along with their own brood. They had been kind and caring. They said he was eleven now and doing very well. They hadn't adopted him and he had kept his mother's name.

Darcy had put on some weight and gray had taken over much of her long blonde hair, but her beautiful bright blue eyes still shone - as bright as city lights - with her whimsical and loving spirit. Her laughing smile was still the same. We remembered that day long ago in the saloon when we had found that extraordinary connection.

Her husband Henry was bald except for his dark red hair on the sides and back of his head. He was gregarious and had quizzical, kind brown eyes and I knew he was the good man she deserved. Henry Wilcox had made a success in real estate speculation during Denver's growth spurt at the end of the century. Their own property was spacious and a fine looking parcel of land.

As it turned out for reasons I am about to tell you, I stayed a few days at Henry and Darcy's place. I was a welcomed friend.

Darcy led me by the hand, her sensual touch still as soft as goose down, and said for me to come out back of the house. She wanted me to see the children playing out in the field. My mind was overwhelmed as the strong feelings I felt that day ago past surged in my heart again as though it had been a moment ago.

She explained how industrious they had been mowing a large area of the hay field, cultivating a fine lawn and building a wondrous green baseball field. Henry was a fan of the game and invested in his very own professional baseball park.

When she led me to the baseball field and spoke softly about the boy, I remembered again how I had thought about her and her voice as sweet as the sugar candy. I was so happy she had Henry. She was such a fine woman; she deserved not to go to waste.

Darcy pointed to a tall boy, with brown eyes and hair, playing center field. She motioned to him to come over to us. It was a practice game so he didn't mind and trotted over to where we were standing with his center fielder's glove on his left hand. She introduced him to me and he smiled at me quizzically. How fitting this was for both her and me.

So I found you David McAuley. That is the rest of my story – many parts my father Morgan, my brother in spirit Josiah and your mother Fannie never knew. I loved your mother better than any woman in my life. I have tried to live an honorable life and do the right thing.

Once in a lifetime if he is lucky, a man meets a woman like your mother. She was extraordinary in so many ways, I cannot tell you. But know that I loved her and knew her well. I can feel her with me always in spirit if never again in body.

Your mother told me that if you can have both love and duty, you have grace within you. I believe she had both of these things and did have grace.

I never could live up to the duty part, so I fell short of having the grace she had. Duty is washing dirty dishes or dirty hands and doing the things that are necessary and responsible. I had enough of that during the war when I didn't understand duty or what I signed up for would entail. But I have always respected the sense and action of duty in others.

I lived an outdoor physical life – building, making, fighting - which is a hard one but what I chose. I have always kept company with strong, vital men and women – strong in body and spirit. For most of my life, I tried to understand my nature.

My father couldn't explain it to me when I was young. He cared about other things. Your mother brought me to understand it finally in my old age. And now I have made certain that you can know it. It is important because you will understand so many things about yourself better someday.

There is more to this story you will know someday when you are older, but for now you know who I am and where I came from. Now you know that son.

All that you are, all you will ever be, comes from this story. It is your legacy, your heritage, the spirit of your future – your own story that will reveal itself to you one day.

There is one more thing I want to tell you before I go. It is getting dark now. There is just you and me on the field. Pick up your bat and look out at the field. The field lives and breathes just like we do. Men have met on the field to do battle for all of time. They are all there but you can't see them. Just look at the field.

Lay the bat on your shoulder and swing it at the ball. Doesn't matter if there is no ball coming at you. Feel it? Do you think you can hit the ball out of the park? Can you win?

You can if you find your authentic swing. Every one of us has one. Yours is just yours and no one else's. Swing harder. Give it all you got. Hit another one.

Your swing is yours alone and something that can't be taught or learned. It has got to be remembered. The world can rob you of it from all our woulda's and coulda's and shoulda's. Some of us forget what our swing was like. Inside every one of us is one true, authentic swing.

Just swing the bat. Feel the night breeze. Close your eyes. Feel the bat. Feel the weight of it. Don't worry about where the ball is going to go. You can't drive it over the fence. You have to let it. Keep swinging the bat until you are a part of the whole thing. It is something you were born with. That is good. Can you see it? They say God is happiest when his children are at play.

Have you ever watched the best hitter on your team, or opposing team or at a professional game, watched him take a practice swing? Looks like he is searching for something. Then he finds it. He settles. Feel his focus? He hits it right over the fence. He can choose from a lot of swings – strikes, whiffs, bunts, fouls. But there is only one hit in perfect harmony with the field. One hit that is his authentic hit. It chooses him. There is a perfect shot trying to find you. All you got to do is get out of its way.

Look at him. See how he is in the field. Not with intensity as if to slay a dragon. He looks with soft eyes. He sees the place where all the tides, the snow-capped mountains, the seasons and the turning of the earth come together. The place where everything is one, commensurate with your capacity to wonder.

You've got to seek that place with your soul David. Seek it with your hands that are wiser than your head. I can't do it for you. But I hope I can help you find a way- the harmony with the field, your authentic swing, that fence, all that you are.

Well it's getting full dark now and the stars are comin' out. We better go in the house. They will be expectin' us for supper.

───────────── ⫸◦⫷ ─────────────

Darcy and Henry had me stay a few days there. They wanted me to spend all the time with the boy I could. It was a blissful poignant time together with him. They were busy with their chores and their children.

David and I spent long hours on the porch staring at the Rockies. I gave him a pocket knife like mine and we whittled sticks for hours to pass the time. We made a lot of toothpicks and got to know each other warmly and comfortably.

It became time to go and I saddled up Maxine with my blanket roll and looked back a moment more at a loved one once again as I left Denver to go back to Aspen.

A while back before that I had been settled in my place on the slope out of town. The winter of 1898 had come on early and strong. During the storms I stayed snug and warm in my cabin with the woodstove stoked with firewood, isolated and secluded in my solitude – alone but not lonely. I began writin' a book – this one you are reading. I called it *The American: A Man's Life* and it was my story, what I had seen and done. Much of it is and will be about Fannie.

One day I received a letter from Darcy – long after Fannie had passed and just after I got back from visiting there. She wrote me:

June 18, 1899

Dearest David,

We didn't git to talk about this. The years you were gone me and Fannie became best friends. I loved her and looked up to her like an older sister.

You know I was with her when she got sick and agreed to take her son in when she was dyin'.

All the years you were apart, she had kept a diary. I'm sendin' it here to you, but please send it back when you are done with it. Your son David needs to have it to remember his Mama.

I think of you and her all the time, especially when I look at this growin' boy. He is becoming a handsome young man we can be proud of.

Stay well my dear man,

Darcy

Right now I had nearly finished my writin' about my Fannie and my heart leapt when I saw this. I put down the letter on the table and opened the rest of the package. There was a handsome, leather-bound book with a brass clasp. I held it in my hands spellbound, excited and so profoundly sad, my hands trembled and my eyes looked at this treasure through misty tears. I undid the clasp and opened it up.

Here was her story for her son and this part I want to tell you:

My life was a struggle and a joy. My husband Angus and me saw all the trouble in Kentucky and more than we wanted to handle. The Civil War wasn't our fight.

He was a tough son-of-a-bitch and I was no lady. The Lords and Ladies of the Manor, they stayed back in the old country.

As far as my folks, I got kin in West Virginia – they's coal minin' mountain people, and some in upstate New York of all things. They, the West Virginia ones, broke away from the Virginia people because they knew slavery was a sin before God. The Yankees in New York married Irish. It's a good thing my daddy back in Scotland never knew about those ones. He's got no love for Popery. So we's God lovin' Presbyterians by heritage, but now a lotta country Baptists here in America.

Angus's kin, the McAuleys, were close allies with the McGregors until the awful Campbells swallowed up both those clans. Angus's folks got no love for the English and they were cautious about the Irish too.

We can forget about all that old world rivalry. We got our own problems here in America. There are good and bad people everywhere, but we's good at sortin' them out. Now out in the West we call that horse sense.

We moved the hell out of there and come to Colorado. We worked our asses off and made a fine ranch raisin' thoroughbred mustang crossbreeds.

But he died and I was left on my own. At first I wanted to give it up. Then I decided there was no good reason on God's earth I should up and quit this. So I went it alone and hired a couple men to help with the ranchin' work.

Along comes this handsome older middle age man one day. He walks right up to me and says Darcy sent him to look at horses. I had been grievin' for Angus for a long while, but my heart went all aflutter. It had been many years since I felt like that from the sight of a man.

But this man was extraordinary. Not just the sight and scent of him standing there in his sweaty shirt and dusty boots, but even more I sensed a quality.

David Wexley stayed. I showed him horses and we talked. He stayed longer until we fell in love. We talked, we made love 'til the cows came home, ate together and talked some more.

His experiences had been even tougher than mine. I tried to console him, cradle him, mother him. We needed each other.

He stayed. He taught me how to shoot. I taught him how to raise, break and train horses. We loved and loved with our whole selves for two seasons.

He read me poetry. I read him the bible and taught him to pray. He learned he was forgiven. He learned he was not alone.

But this lonesome cowboy couldn't sit still for too long and I knew it. He had dreams and always had this faraway look like he wondered what was over the horizon. I could see it comin'. I knew someday soon I would have to let him go. He needed to fly with his healed wings. I needed to raise my two hands to the sky and watch him climb away out of my sight and my life.

He saddled up and went one day. The sight of him will never leave me as long as I live.

In the spring I had his baby boy. Darcy come over and helped me manage the baby and keep my place runnin'. She had her brood growin' up and the older ones come and helped too.

I told Darcy I miss David. It was the toughest Goddamn thing I ever did in my life lettin' him go. I loved him that much – lettin' him leave, leavin' him his freedom. Still do. Always will.

But I have his son and mine and that is a blessing from God. I haven't lost my faith in Him.

I gently put the diary down on the table next to the letter. There was much more to read but this was all I could bear today. I would treasure her words, see her face in front of my mind's eye, love her forever and pray to the Lord we could be together someday again.

Another day I read the rest of the pages. And then the pages were blank for half of the book. I closed it and held it on my lap for the rest of the afternoon and stared out the window at the cloudless blue sky fading as the sun settled down over the west of the slope. There was a brilliance, like a lambency, almost like gold.

I prayed a prayer of thanksgiving to Him who made us.

Never believe an old man if he tells you he has no regrets about the life he lived or the things he done. We have to do the best we can and answer for the rest of it on the day of reckoning.

_____ end _____

Epilogue

In June of 1900, with the foothills of the Rockies in full bloom and snow capping the peaks, the explosion at the Bear Mountain mine rocked the solid ground in the yards and dropped tons of rock into the mine shaft one hundred feet away from where David and his crew were rebuilding some buttressing members in the tunnel. It caught them completely by surprise since no detonation had been scheduled for that morning. They were located closer to the mine entrance than the point where it occurred, and so they had a slim chance to escape. There were seven of them in all.

Three managed to dash outside to safety and four were crushed by the flying rock and concussion of the explosion. David couldn't run as fast as the younger men but his position was fortunately closer to the entrance than most of his crew. He was the third and the last, after Frank and Henry, to get outside. Fortunately Joe was in the forest cutting timber.

Dazed and blinded in the bright sunlight, David watched to see if anymore would come out behind him. None did.

A man watched from a spot on high ground about one hundred fifty yards from the tunnel entrance. In the confusion, no one noticed him standing alone as a stranger. He was a Mexican and a big man. He had come all this way from Sonora because his brother had been killed years ago in Hermosillo.

The Mexican was surprised to see David come out. He had planned for the explosion to kill him. But he had waited and watched for the result and had a contingency plan. He took careful aim with his repeater rifle and fired a 30 caliber bullet through David's back. It pierced his heart and David fell instantly. No one heard the rifle report or realized what had happened in those chaotic moments of noise and confusion.

He had died in summertime as he had wished but not by the peaceful means he had hoped for. There was no heir to carry on the Wexley name but there was a son all the same.

David passed out of his body and floated toward the bright light. The faces of Darcy and his young son standing beside Josiah, Mary, David and Josena Ashford faded as they waved goodbye. Fannie stood before him bathed in white light, smiling and beckoning him toward the place where he was welcomed. We do not walk alone.

Mary, Josiah's wife, had read about it in the newspaper back east in Ohio. All the report said was that there had been an accident at the Bear Mountain mine in Aspen, Colorado. When she told Josiah, they contacted the mining company for they had known it was the last mine he had worked for. They learned that David had been killed there but the circumstances were not clear.

Grief-stricken and shocked, Josiah arranged to bring his body back to Hamilton for burial on his land. It took a few days before he met the train in Cincinnati and brought the casket home in his wagon.

Josiah dedicated a cemetery and memorial park in Ashford, Ohio. He had provided a vast parcel of cultivated land for the internment of former slaves and Union and Confederate soldiers of the Civil War and their descendants.

He gave the eulogy for David's re-internment memorial service there after moving his remains from the back lot of his home. He, and members of his family, would follow them and him to this place in the future.

It was a peaceful, beautiful green space with rolling hills, tree-shaded valleys, babbling brooks and monuments of forgiveness, understanding, remembrance and healing for all the American people.

Frank, Henry and Joe, David's men that had survived the tragedy, took Maxine into their care. She was kept at the town livery. Folks could tell she was grieving; knew David was gone. She left most of her feed. Folks were waiting and trying to decide what to do. They were good people and nobody was going to steal her.

Darcy and Henry Wilcox heard about it and immediately agreed to go to Aspen and get Maxine. When they arrived in town they found her right away and explained to those who cared what they intended to do. They would bring her home.

The old girl was past middle age but still had a lot of life in her. They brought her back to Denver to their place, not very far from where she was born. Maxine recognized that.

Maxine had a sense, maybe from smell or somehow, that young David was David. She followed him all around the corral inside the paddock and David understood too the meaning of this. He fed her carrots and apples. They grieved together and had each other. She lived out the rest of her days happy there with young David riding her around their paddock.

Old Josiah died later in 1906 and Mary followed him in 1917.

David had written a letter from Aspen to Joe in the late fall of 1899, after many years had passed in their correspondence.

November 10, 1899

My Dear Brother Josiah,

I have found a son I never knew I had. He lives in Denver with a dear friend and her husband. He is an eleven year old spittin' image of me. My love, his mother, had died some few years before, but I was in Aspen and lost touch. My woman Fannie McAuley named him David.

It was best that my friends raised him instead of me after Fannie died. They had been caring for him so well and faithfully for so long.

As one who loves you, I have always remained grateful that you had your Mary, your woman who healed your sorrows. My Fannie did that for me and I have forgiven myself for my past.

The melancholy that remains is that I could not stay with her forever. I had to remain true to myself. But my love remains forever and in her next life she knows that.

You can rest assured the weight of your concerns for me can be lifted from your heart.

I still miss you and your family, our days in the South and all those years together up in Ohio.

As you would know, I have had a lot of years to think about our past. The true emancipation that followed the war, not the Emancipation Proclamation before it which was a political artifice to help the Union war effort, was the change to the Constitution which was a sin. It was a shameful sin because there was no effective plan or actions before it or after it to put the Negro on a footing where he could survive and thrive as a human being in America.

I blame the politicians and the American people for that. The Abolitionists and the Firebrands made no accommodation. The Freedman's Bureau was too little too late. It will be a problem for the black man and the white man for the next hundred years. I know you understand this as well or better than I. You have spent your life as a legislator trying to find a path forward for all Americans.

Joe, I wrote a book out here in Aspen. It is about my life in the West and my whole life before that including my time with you. I called it "The American: A Man's Life" and I found a print shop in town to bind up a few copies. I began writing it up here in my cabin before I ever met my son and then I finished it up after that *and meant it for him. Darcy Farrow Wilcox in Denver has it for him for when he is grown up.*

I still see the starved spirits of the apparitions from thirty five years ago. Not from the long marches or the fighting, the waiting in camps or the prisons, but the dead that haven't crossed over still, their spirits not resolved, their work undone.

I tell them now to be at peace as I am. There is beauty yet undiscovered, its cause worth the toil and the sorrow, its love the promise kept. I no longer regret it, my life the richer for the discovery of the child born from its passion, from the love of a woman, from the sight of God through her eyes and her promise of the life thereafter, the truth in immortality assured. My soul is full of love just as I know yours is. I can see it now Joe. It had been a grand time and the glory is not in the past. It is yet to come.

Be well my brother until we meet again,

David

Joe wrote back later that month with a tenderness of understanding:

November 30, 1899

My Dearest David,

I understand the mixture of your grief and happiness more than you can possibly know.

We were together when we looked for my Josena. We were together when we learned she had been killed. We were together when we learned of my lost daughter but couldn't find her.

But we were apart when my grown children found her in Mississippi and brought her home a middle aged woman – my daughter Hanna Drish.

Our lives have continued to follow together in Providence's divine path.

Your insights about our country have a depth very few can appreciate or understand. But you know I do brother.

Please send me a copy of your book so that my children will always remember you.

Forever your brother,

Joe

The strong bond of their lives had continued to entwine them and connect them together after the visible connection between them had been broken over time and distance, but had been replaced by the invisible hand.

Josiah's son, David Ashford had read David Wexley's journals left for his father's safekeeping and the book he had left as his legacy. He had known his father's friend when he was young and David Wexley had lived beside them. David Ashford showed the journals to his son, Josiah Ashford II and explained what this man had meant to his grandfather, what these two men had meant to each other, what it had meant to their family, that David Wexley had left behind a son, that while his grandfather and David Wexley were gone, there was a part of them still left behind.

In 1955, in Montgomery, Alabama, a forty year old man from Hamilton, Ohio named Josiah Ashford II, met a sixty-five year old man from Denver, Colorado named David McAuley. They marched down the street locked arm in arm together.

Martin had told them, "The time is always right to do what is right."

Josiah and David were free men who learned about their human connection. Their common ground had begun ninety years ago by the Mississippi River in Natchez when one's grandfather had met one's father. The ancient tree of their family history had common roots tracing way back to Africa and Scotland.

They had come from the same place as hard-bitten, God loving freedom fighters. They knew where they came from and knew their purpose. They knew their authentic selves. They faced the world on their feet, never bowed down or backed up.

The circle is unbroken and the American story continues.

———————————⟶◦⟵———————————

There is no need to pray for the forgiveness of the sins of those that came before. He has forgiven them. There is no need to pray for their protection or safety. They have been gathered together with all those who love them, enfolded in His loving arms. We need only to remember them and honor them with our love and gratitude for their just duty and sacrifice.

So that we may never forget him or the many others who have served and have given their last full measure of devotion, who lived on to the end of the time given them, or died in the moment of service, who must be honored and remembered to the end of our time, and by all those who follow us, here are words better than I could ever express them from the old book:

All these were honoured in their generations

And were the glory of their times

There be of them that have left a name behind them

That their praises might be reported

And some there be which have no memorial

Who are perished as though they had never been

And are become as though they had never been born

And their children after them

But these were merciful men

Whose richeousness hath not been forgotten

With their seed shall continually remain

A good inheritance and their children are within the covenant

Their seed standeth fast and their children for their sakes

Their seed shall remain for ever

And their glory shall not be blotted out

Their bodies are buried in peace

But their name liveth for evermore

Ecclesiasticus, chapter 44, excerpt

Author's Footnote

I owe a special debt of gratitude to Canadian musical artists Ian Tyson and Sylvia Fricker Tyson. Their evocative voices told the emotional stories that helped me visualize and internalize the American West and its people back in those days. They deeply influenced my insights and made it feel as though I was there with my characters.

When I visited Scotland in 2006, we went to the Edinburgh castle on top of the hill, overlooking the modern city and the Firth of Forth toward the North Sea. It was noon at the end of May and a warm day. The Sargent-at-Arms ordered the firing of the cannon at the parapets on the top of the castle.

It was a tradition kept for all the years of their history. The cannon was fired every noon as a small ceremony. The guide told us it was to insure that the cannon was in good working order so that if the English come, we will be ready. Despite their loyalty to the U.K., their avowed British citizenship, the years of peaceful cooperation, the centuries of growth to their modernity, they would never be English and their Scottish spirit would never be lost.

This pride in tradition, this self-reliant, independent spirit is the same that built my country. The pioneers that built America brought this spirit and its ancient traditions with them. They were the men and women that conquered and settled our continent and they are the people who gave us our American spirit. We face the world on our feet, we never bow down to nobility; we endure; we never back down; we do what is right.

We fiercely hold to an egalitarian view toward our fellow man based on the idea that no man is our superior or our authority. We are Americans.

Characters in order of appearance

David Wexley

Josiah Ashford

Darcy Farrow

Fannie McAuley

Maxine

Rosa

Maria

Jeff Grady

Frank Dell

John Knowland

Sam Mc Nabb

Joe Johnson

Earl Thomas

Henry Wallace

James Longstreet

Henry Wilcox

David McAuley

Josiah Ashford II

Locations

Hamilton, Ohio

Chicago, Illinois

Denver, Colorado

Aspen, Colorado

Santa Fe, New Mexico

El Paso, Texas

Hermosillo, Sonora, Mexico

Montgomery, Alabama

Timeline

1832 – Born in Baltimore, Maryland

1848 – Sailed topsail schooners

1862 – Fought in battle of Antietam

1864 – Fought in Battle of the Wilderness

1864 – Imprisoned in Andersonville, Georgia

1865 – Came to Ohio with Josiah

1873 – Economic Panic, Grant's 2nd term

1887 – Left Ohio (age 55) to go west, stopped in Chicago

1888- Met Fannie and stayed in Denver

1889 – Moved to Aspen

1889- 1898- Travel through New Mexico, Texas, Mexico

1893 – Chicago World's Fair and Columbia Exposition

1893 – Economic Panic, railroad over-speculation

1896- Gunfight in Hermosillo

1899- Visited Denver

1900 – Killed at the mine (age 68)

1900 – Casket brought back to Cincinnati on the train

Review of books by Mr. Jennings

Hanna's Promise

It's a heartfelt and inspiring story of love, devotion and faith. One that the author weaves the sorrows, the triumphs, and the majestic harmony of God's grace through the wonderful and heart wrenching circumstances. Hanna sees the world through her own eyes, and sees the goodness in all people no matter of race or of circumstances. She sets out to bring hope and grace to everyone.

The author is a gifted writer and story teller. Hanna's Promise is more than just a book. It's a work of grace itself, one that every person should slow down long enough to read and enjoy it.

Toni House, author
Baton Rouge, LA

Hanna's Promise is David Claire Jennings second historical fiction novel. It is the sequel to After Bondage and War published last year. Intertwining historical events and sometimes little known facts within the story of Hanna, an orphaned slave girl, makes for fascinating reading. The reader enters the post-Civil War era and follows the life and times of Hanna Drish and the family she never knew.

The end of the Civil War finds 8 year old Hanna newly orphaned and suddenly a freed slave. Fortunately she is loved by John and Sarah Drish, who although her masters, love her as their own. With the threat of invading Union armies, they take Hanna to live with their friends in Mobile. We get a different view of slave owners than the usual stereotype as we come to know the two former slave owners who raise Hanna and care for her as a member of their family.

Hanna never knew her father, as he never knew of her until after the Civil War ended. He had gone on to become a renowned state representative in Ohio, remarried and had twins, one named for his dead wife, and one for his best friend, a Union soldier he met after the war. The novel After Bondage and War tells the poignant story of these two men and their search for happiness and peace.

Hanna's Promise is filled with the spiritual relationship she has with the Archangel Michael who helps her achieve a life of hope and grace through her relationships with everyone she meets. As she travels through life she meets many challenges as any Negro in the post-Civil War south would. But her serenity and kindness always shine through and help her overcome the negativity she encounters.

The reader is thrilled when she is finally united with the family she never knew and goes on to lead a blessed life affecting everyone she meets.

This is a book that engages the reader in the lives of the characters and leaves them with a feeling of hope for the future of mankind.

Irene Havekost – 6/4/16

I bought *Hanna's Promise- A Story of Grace and Hope* because the title intrigued me. As I began to read the characters came to life, perhaps because I am an adopted child who was reunited with his siblings. The twins David and Josena were described so that I felt that I could see them in my mind. The journey they took to find their sister was hauntingly familiar to my own journey. Hanna's struggles and her devotion to her promise to God often brought tears to my eyes.

David Claire Jennings writing was easy to understand, yet the words he used were powerful and capable of evoking strong emotion in the reader. The history was fascinating and full of things that I never learned in school. It gave me a better picture of life in the south after the Civil War.

I became so involved with the story and the characters that I wanted to know more about what had happened prior to the time of this book, so I purchased *After Bondage and War* by Mr. Jennings. I can't wait to start it and find out what happened.

I heartily recommend this book to anyone who has an interest in history, and likes characters that show the goodness in people and who lead lives of importance to others.

Thomas David

Hanna's Promise by David Claire Jennings was a very touching story for me; if you like historical fiction with a spiritual twist, you'll like this book. It's not a very difficult read, and it flows very smoothly between the stories of David Ashford and his twin sister Josena, who are secondary protagonists and second generation returning characters from David's first novel, After Bondage and War. The time period is post Civil War and Reconstruction.

David and Josena are son and daughter to Josiah Ashford, also a returning character; unlike David's first novel, Josiah plays a secondary role to David and Josena. Josena and David have spiritual and intellectual similarities, albeit one was trained as a historian and war correspondent and the other as an anthropologist. However, the physical characteristics and personality differences between the two are charmingly demonstrated: "Together they reminded you of Abraham and Mary Todd Lincoln, had they not been a brother and sister of color from a more modern time."

The meat and potatoes of this novel is David and Josena's quest to find their long-lost sister, an enigmatic woman who was the child of their father Josiah Ashford, when he was still in bondage, and his then wife, also a slave, named Josena, from whom his daughter from his second marriage is named after. We revisit the tragic slave revolt, briefly mentioned in After Bondage and War, and learn more details about how Josiah's wife Josena was killed. David and Josena's quest for their long-lost sister compels the reader to read on as both the reader and David and Josena learn more details about their sister: they find out her name is Hanna.

Hanna is the third-introduced, but main protagonist of the novel. Hanna's upbringing is skillfully portrayed: she is raised by two benevolent white families, the first, named the Drishes, had to give her up when the Civil War came calling too close to and even threatened their home, and the second, the Blanchards. Both families loved her like a daughter. The idea that a slaveholding white family could love and care for Hanna as a daughter is the first glimpse of racial harmony in the book. This theme of racial harmony is apparent throughout the book, especially with the character of Hanna, and it is a theme so desperately lacking in today's modern time.

Hanna's character is revealed to have a very spiritual mission. Her impetus in life is to promote racial harmony and further it through love, caring for all people, kindness and as the author puts it: "act justly, love mercy, and walk humbly with her God." Hanna's mission is introduced through a visit from an angel early on in the novel, in her childhood; she is asked to make a covenant, a promise to God to further racial harmony. It is this covenant, this promise that lends the book its name, Hanna's Promise.

All in all, this is a very good read. The language is easy to read, not highfalutin, but the concepts and themes are very deep and spiritual. Civil War and Reconstruction historical references abound. The characters are a joy to discover. God Himself even plays a role. And the quest of David and Josena to find their long-lost sister draws the reader in and compels them to feel the joy of their discovery. Hanna's spiritual quest for racial harmony is also very deep and her vision of a better America through spirituality, kindness, sympathy, empathy, love and caring is a quest that we all would do well to emulate today.

Edwin Smith

After Bondage and War

I first met David Claire Jennings when he was a student in my History 121 course at Columbia College. I soon discovered that I had much more to learn from him than I could ever possibly teach him. Much like the characters David Wexley and Josiah Ashford in After Bondage and War, David and I were at two different places in our lives. Yet, like Wexley and Ashford we discovered a bond and formed a lasting friendship.

David's passion for writing, combined with his very practical understanding of history and his life experiences all come together in his first book: After Bondage and War. David tells the story of slavery, war, and reconciliation with a level of emotion often absent from writing; he tells the human side.

James Giannettino, Jr., adjunct history professor, Columbia College

---

After Bondage and War is David Claire Jennings first historical fiction novel. It is the poignant and touching story of two men from entirely different backgrounds who meet after the Civil War, form a bond of friendship and brotherhood which last a lifetime. Josiah Ashford is a slave in Alabama, while David Wexley is an outspoken and adventurous Union soldier who had just endured the horrors of captivity at Andersonville. The war is over, but for these two men, the journey is just beginning.

Through fate or divine intervention, they meet in Natchez, are immediately drawn to each other, and begin a life-long adventure as they struggle to find the peace and happiness they both so desperately want and need.

Aside from their color, the main difference in Josiah and David is their faith. Josiah is filled with it, and David is searching for it. Looking for their place in this new world, they travel through the south looking for Josiah's wife Josena and when the search ends in tragedy, they head north to Ohio to make a new life.

For the reader, the fictional story is set in and among historical events, all true but with added insights into the hearts and minds of many famous men of the time. For a history buff, the story only adds to the history told throughout the book. For the fiction buff, the history only adds reality and interesting and many unknown facts to a wonderful story.

The book is an easy read, the reader is never mired down in long historical diatribes, and the fictional characters stories flow effortlessly from one situation to another.

Irene Havekost

_____

Dave has a unique gift for writing history. He also has great perspective on life in general.

Dave is one of those people who has not only seen life, managed to live through those many ups and downs which we humans share but taken the time to observe and chronicle his perspectives.

William Burak, adjunct history professor, Columbia College

Not being a fan of history, **After Bondage and War** is not a book I would have picked off the shelf. However, a friend recommended it and to make him happy, I bought the book.

Surprisingly, I found it to be very good. There was just enough history with many things I had never known, to keep me reading on to discover what happened to the many characters in the story. Having been born and raised in the north, but spending the majority of my life in the south, it was easy to see the truth in the descriptions of places, attitudes and actions in the story.

I found myself relating to David Wexley's search for happiness and faith and envious of Josiah's deeply ingrained faith. The story was interesting, the characters likable or unlikable enough to keep my interest from beginning to end.

I look forward to the sequel Hanna's Promise to see where the story leads.

Dennis Owen – 6/4/16

I read *After Bondage and War* because I wanted to find out the story behind Hanna Drish, the heroine in *Hanna's Promise*. David Claire Jennings first book lived up to the challenge. I enjoyed it as much if not more than *Hanna's Promise*. As a replanted northerner, I think that I now finally understand the strong feelings surrounding the Civil War that still exist in the south. The history was fascinating, there was so much detail about historical figures that I knew them personally, how they thought and how they felt.

As I followed the life stories of the two main characters, Josiah Ashford and David Wexley, they became my friends. I suffered with them in their defeats and celebrated with them in their triumphs. I have always believed in the goodness of people, and to see two men from different walks of life, bond together as brothers to survive and succeed in the world, made my heart sing with happiness. Their story was touching, poignant and a testament to the concept of brotherhood among all men.

I am not an avid reader, so it is unusual for me to have quickly read and thoroughly enjoyed two books in a short period of time. Both books by Mr. Jennings had an easy reading style. Not too filled with long descriptive sentences, but with a structure that gave me as a reader many an "aha" moment. I felt treated as an intelligent reader who would understand the nuances of what was going on without being hit over the head with the information.

I heartily recommend *After Bondage and War* to any reader who enjoys a great story, truly believable and likable characters, and thought provoking ideas all mixed in with interesting historical information. I look forward to any future books by David Claire Jennings.

Thomas David

David Claire Jennings' novel After Bondage and War deals is a very touching story that deals with the underlying theme of racial harmony, as evidenced by the friendship of two characters from very disparate backgrounds, a white Union soldier with post-traumatic stress after the Civil War and a newly freed slave from a Southern plantation.

The two main characters and protagonists in this novel are Josiah Ashford and David Wexley. Josiah Ashford is poignantly described as having an "insatiable curiosity and an African respect and reverence for the wisdom of his elders...As an adult, he came to the view that he was the master of his fate. Free will permitted him to take charge of his life and strive for his own betterment."

David Wexley was born into a well-to-do family, but longed for adventure. Not wanting to continue in his father's business, he worked as a merchant marine for a while, in order to fulfill his wanderlust. Under a romantic view of war, he later joins up with the Union army during the Civil War, having viewed slavery as an injustice. The thrust of his character is a passion for fighting injustice due to his Scots-Irish temperament. Briefly, and beautifully, describing David's temperament due to his Scots-Irish roots: "They had a long history of hating the English but would pick a fight with anybody if the cause was right..."

The main antagonists in this novel are Marcus Taylor and Rebecca Stanley, slaveholders of the South. Exquisitely written, we learn of their ensuing courtship, marriage, and establishment of a plantation. Marcus and Rebecca acquire Josiah as one of their slaves; we learn of his harsh treatment on the plantation by Marcus' overseer, and Josiah's tender love for, and subsequent marriage to, another slave named Josena. We also learn of Josena's tragic fate.

As a historical fiction novel, After Bondage and War is about a 50/50 percent blend of actual historical events and characters versus fictional events and characters. Fans of Michael and Jeff Shaara and John Jakes will enjoy this novel. The 50/50 blend makes David Claire Jennings rather unique as an author, as the Shaaras and John Jakes have a higher percentage of either actual historical or fictional events and characters.

Civil War historians will enjoy the military strategy and history depicted in the chapters devoted to David Wexley's battles in the Civil War. But the humanity of the War is never lost:

"As darkness fell, he lay on the field with the thousands of the dead and wounded. It was quiet after the cannon and muskets had ceased firing. The ghosts kept company with the wounded and suffering. It was so still. There was only the sounds of the moans and cries for help from the living and those still to die."

It is a chance – or was it God's Divine Providence? - meeting in Natchez between the newly freed slave Josiah Ashford and the newly released from Andersonville prison Union soldier David Wexley that forms the critical turning point in the novel. Each side has to overcome their fear of how they will be received by the other, and the eventual outcome is a great success – they become fast friends and travelling companions.

The novel ends with the subsequent generations of Josiah's offspring, and David Wexley leaves to go out West. What happens to Josiah's children? – stay tuned for David Claire Jennings' second novel Hanna's Promise! What happens to David Wexley? – stay tuned for the third book in the saga, The American!

Edwin Smith

───────────────────────────────────